Lock Down Publications and Ca$h
Presents

IF YOU CROSS ME ONCE 5

Vengeance Is Mine

D1714177

Written By

Anthony Fields

OCT - - 2024

First Edition 2024

Printed in the United States of America

Lock Down Publications
P.O. Box 944
Stockbridge, GA 30281
www.lockdownpublications.com

Like our page on Facebook: Lock Down Publications
www.facebook.com/lockdownpublications.ldp

Stay Connected with Us!

Text **LOCKDOWN** to 22828 to stay up-to-date with new releases, sneak peaks, contests and more…

Like our page on Facebook:
Lock Down Publications

Join Lock Down Publications/The New Era Reading Group

Visit our website:
www.lockdownpublications.com

Follow us on Instagram:
Lock Down Publications

Email Us: We want to hear from you!

Dedication

This book is dedicated to the millions of men and women incarcerated in the United States. I do this to entertain you, even if it's only for a little while.

Acknowledgements

All praise is due to Allah, the lord of all the worlds. Without his mercy, I would have been dead years ago. With that said, let me just say that I appreciate all the people who have supported my career over the years and purchased every novel that I wrote. Well, even if you only purchased one book... Thank you. Thank you to all the bookstores, vendors, websites, and individual book sellers that moved my product. Thank you to all the book clubs that supported me with the emergence of social media. It's surprising that we don't see or hear from book clubs like we used to. That's not good. We need to bring back and support OOSA (Only One Stop Away) and Sistas of Lit and the many other book clubs that used to rule. Thank you to Toni McDaniel, a member of OOSA that did so much to further my career. I will never forget what you did for me. Can't you tell? I'm still acknowledging you and we have spoken in about ten years. Over the course of my literary career, I've said bad things about a lot of people. I wanted to be the 50 cent of the book industry. But that phase in my life has passed. I'm wiser and more humble now. I'm smarter and even more ambitious. Before I get into what my ambitions are, let me say thank you to Teri Woods and Lucas Riggins. Let me say thank you to Wahida Clark who took the time out to write to me and mentor me while she was still in prison. Then once she came home and got on her feet, she grabbed me out of the ashes and put me one when nobody else would. Although our relationship soured over time when greed entered the picture, I still gotta say thank you for all you did to get my name out there to the people. Thank you. There's really no need to thank T. Styles and the Cartel publications, but I will anyway because before things went bad, at least you acknowledged a sick pen game and the talent in me. That motivated me, so thank you to you and Cherisse Washington. Thank you to Crystal Perkins-Stell for the little you did to advance my career. And please stop exploiting the ignorance of incarcerated men and women. At least keep it one hundred with them and tell them that most of the services you provide for them are free on line. Get your money, but not off the backs of the marginalized and naive. To NeNe Capri, thank you for all the conversations we had and all the knowledge you gave me when I started NDA Streets Publishing. Thank you for showing me around Georgia and all the extra things you did to make my stay in Atlanta enjoyable. Thank you to Cash and Lockdown Publications for giving me yet another platform to get my thoughts to the people.

Okay, now back to my ambitions. I want to branch out into other genres of books. I want to turn my books into TV series and movies. Shout out to Kwame Teague and Carl Weber. Erick S. Gray and TuShonda Whitaker. Shout out to Manny Halley for what he was able to accomplish in TV and films. Allah willing, I'll be up next to show my abilities in other channels. Shout out to all the people who started this 'If You Cross Me Once' journey with me. I never meant to ride the story out like this. It was only supposed to be two books and here we are at the 5th one. Hopefully, this one will be the last. But y'all know me. Might do some other stuff at the last minute, so just stay tuned. Shout out to Sherina Salomon and friends.

Shout out to all the good men behind the fence who are holding it down. Shout out to all the people in the world holding the good men behind the fence down. Shout out to the fence because although you can hold our bodies, you can't contain our brains. Shout out to all the people I love. You know who you are. Up next are Angel 5, In the Blink of An Eye 2 and AMEEN (the beginning). After that there will be something new. I promise. As always...

DC Stand Up!

Anthony Fields

Chapter 1
Detective Robert 'Bob' Mathis
Homicide Division
Pennsylvania and Branch Ave.

"What was the name of that motel again?"

"Roadway Inn. Sits next to Quality Inn on Allentown Road. But if you're not looking for it you won't see it. Sorta sits off to the side and to the rear. But it shares a parking lot with Quality Inn. Place doesn't have its own entrance point. You have to turn into the Quality Inn parking lot to ride on through to get to the Roadway. Perfect out of the way spot for a double murder," Detective Jake Reese said.

"And you said that Jacob Newsome called it in here?" I asked Jake.

"Yeah. Said that a few of you... *detectives*, were just discussing Maurice Best and then he shows up dead in Prince George's County. Newsome asked to speak to you, but you were busy at the time."

"I can't fuckin' believe it. I kinda knew that eventually someone would get to him but how could he end up with Trina Davis? And why kill her?"

"That's why P.G. County detectives make more money than us, Bob. They get to answer questions like that and have all the fun. Us... on the other hand, we get to investigate five muthafuckas shooting at each other and an eleven-year-old boy ends up being the only person killed. We get to chase fifteen scumbags involved in an intercity neighborhood beef that only manages to kill innocent bystanders, namely little kids. Let Jacob Newsome and his crew determine who and why the notorious Trina Boo and Moe Best were slain together while fucking in a roach motel. We got..." Jake Reese's cell phone rang. He answered the call. "Okay. Be right there in a few. Alright. Goodbye." Jake turned back to me. "See what I mean? A woman's been killed in a parking garage near Gallery Place. We got our own shit to deal with. Moe Best was a great informant but that's over now. He's gone. Time to move on to the next one."

I nodded my head. Jake was right. No need in crying over spilled milk. I stood up from my desk and grabbed my coat. It was time to move on.

***

One... Two... Three... Four... Five... Six... Seven... Eight. I counted the number of shell casings left behind at the scene of the murder. Eight. Eight bullets had been fired into a young woman dressed in a Chipotle uniform, as she tried to get into her car. I stood over the body of what used to be a beautiful girl and my heart sank. The shell casings were forty caliber casings. Any one of those bullets would have killed the young girl if put into the right spot. Eight bullets were definitely overkill. What had the young woman done to deserve such a brutal death? Twenty-one years on the job and that one question will never stop coming to mind. Sometimes, we got to answer the question and sometimes we didn't. I continued to stare at the young woman on the ground. The car she'd been killed next to was a new modeled Infiniti sedan that was registered to her. I held the license and registration for the Infiniti in my hand and looked at the photo on the driver's license for an extended period, then back at the victim on the pavement.

"Bob," Jake Reese called my name and broke my reverie.

"Yeah, Jake?" I replied, eyes still on the woman on the ground.

"Her cellphone was in her pocket. I fished it out and used her thumb to open the phone."

"Somebody somewhere would frown upon you doing that Jake, but so be it. What did you find inside Shontay Dunn's cellphone?"

"Photos that I think you need to see." Jake turned the cellphone to face me. "Recognize that face?"

Grabbing the phone out of Jake's hand, I looked closely at the picture. There were two women in the photo and one of them was Shontay Dunn. The other woman's face looked familiar, but I couldn't place it. The two women looked like twins. They were both smiling. "One of them is the victim…"

"And the other is… *was* a victim. One of ours. She's Raquel Dunn, the woman who was fished out of the Potomac. She'd been stabbed…"

"In both eyes, disemboweled and her throat was cut. I didn't recog… wait, Raquel Dunn was Sean Branch's baby's mother…"

"Say hello then goodbye to their daughter, Shontay Dunn."

"Fuck!" I exclaimed and looked again at the slain woman on the ground. "Somebody just killed Sean Branch's daughter!"

"I'm afraid so, mi amigo." Jake replied.

"Nothing was ever confirmed, but word on the street was that Sean killed Raquel Dunn for not holding him down while he was in prison. There's no way he killed his own daughter."

"I never said he did."

"This has got to be retaliation for something else. Someone else that Sean killed since he's been home."

"Moe Best, maybe. He had what? Four or five brothers? A couple that I hear are also killers. Or one of his nephews.

They've been knee-deep in neighborhood beef with Montana. Sean is from Langdon Park just like the Best clan. The Best family would know all about Sean's daughter and probably where she worked. Trina Boo had a son, too. Maybe he decided to avenge his mom."

"Jake, Sean Branch has killed more people in DC this year than cancer. Whoever shot and killed his daughter could be anyone with any number of reasons why. The streets of our nation's capital are about to be very unsafe for anybody that Sean suspects. God help us all…"

***

The most harrowing part of my job was notifying the next of kin once someone was killed. Especially someone that was only twenty years old. A young woman who had an entire life ahead of her to live, despite the degenerate animal that birthed her. Since I was now investigating Shontay Dunn's murder and I was familiar with all the parents and players involved in the possible saga, I decided to notify Shontay's kin in person and as soon as possible. The address on Shontay Dunn's driver's license was for Sean Branch's mother's house in Langdon Park, blocks away from Moe Best's family home. It was after one in the morning and the lights inside the large, red brick home were out. I exhaled loudly and exited the car. The night air attacked me like an unseen creature. Quickly zipping my parka to the top of my coat, the top layer shielded my neck from the cold. I lowered the North Face beanie on my head to cover my ears. I could feel what felt like snowdrops. At the home's front door, I rang the doorbell twice, then opened the screen door and knocked loudly. Minutes later, a woman's voice filled my ears.

"Who is it? And what the hell do you want?" The woman asked.

"It's the police, ma'am. I need to talk to you," I replied. I could see the face of the woman through the glass on the door. I pulled my detective shield and held it for her to see. That and my identification.

Seconds later, the large wooden front door opened. "Is this about my son? Is Sean dead?"

Looking the woman straight in the eyes, I shook my head. "No, ma'am. This visit isn't about your son Sean. Unfortunately, this visit's about your granddaughter Shontay. She was shot and killed..."

The woman in front of me screamed and dropped to her knees.

***

Thirty minutes later...

Sharon Branch had regained her composure some. She sat on her living room couch hugging herself while still shedding tears that she didn't bother to wipe away. "Please... tell me, what happened to my granddaughter."

I sat on a sofa directly across from her. A small, wooden table sat in between us. I had removed my coat after carrying the woman to the couch after her collapse at the beginning of our conversation. "Shontay had just left work at Chipotle. She was about to enter a vehicle..."

"An Infiniti sedan with paper tags," Sharon Branch said. "Her father just purchased the car for her. Days ago. Do you think it was an attempted carjacking, detective?"

"No, ma'am. Neither was it an attempted robbery. Someone stood a short distance away from her and shot her, then walked up closer and fired some more. This... What happened to Shontay, was personal. Intentional. Planned."

Sharon Branch didn't respond immediately. I let my last words marinate inside her head. The silence between us was now deafening. After several minutes passed, Sharon said, "I always knew a day like this would come. I always knew that police officers would come to my home to tell me that someone had died. Been killed in the streets. But never in my wildest dreams had I ever thought that it would be my granddaughter who'd been killed." Sharon Branch sobbed uncontrollably for minutes before regaining herself. "I always heard about my son and what he did in the streets. I'm not a fool. I know the son I raised. I knew that all the rumors I heard were true although he always lied to me. Sean never admitted to me that he killed anyone. He was just like his father. Everything about him was. Sean inherited every gene that his father had. Right down to the desire to kill people. I was under no illusion as to who my son was; who he still is today. But I sincerely pray that whoever did this to my grandbaby has made their peace with God. Because in a few minutes, I'm gonna have to call Sean and tell him about his daughter. His only child. I'm gonna cry the entire time while doing it and that in itself is gonna light a fire inside of him. Then to hear that Shontay has been... has been..." Sharon broke down again. "Sean doesn't love a lot in this world. He loved his father who was killed in prison when he was ten. He loved the man who came into his life after his father, a man that I loved named Ameen Bashir who was killed when Sean was thirteen or fourteen, I believe. He loved Raquel Dunn, Shontay's mother. Somebody killed her last year. He loves his mother. But he loved his daughter more than anybody. Some people say that Sean is an animal. That he kills people with reckless abandon. They call him remorseless, heartless and cruel. I've heard the word barbaric associated with him. And words like psychopathic, demonic and callous. But none of those words will be enough to describe what the world is about to see. Sean has been home for almost seven or eight months and there have been bodies found and unfound that people have attributed to my son. The latest one being Maurice Best and that girl that was killed with him out in Maryland. Those murders are about to pale in comparison to the ones about to be committed once Sean learns that Shontay is gone. Detective... Can you pray with me?"

Pray? I was caught off guard by the request. I'd delivered news to notify hundreds of victims next of kins, but I'd never been asked to pray with anyone. I wasn't really a religious man, but I saw no harm in honoring a bereaved woman's request to talk to God. "You want me to pray with you?"

"Yes, detective." Sharon Branch said. "I want to pray for the soul of my granddaughter and the souls of all the people that are about to die at the hands of her father. And I don't want to do that alone." Sharon Branch got up from her seat on the couch and walked over to me. She grabbed my hand and pulled until I stood up.

"Dear heavenly father..."

Chapter 2
Sean Branch

The loud sounds of a cell phone vibrating near me woke me from my slumber. I reached out my hand to silence the noise and inadvertently knocked the phone off the nightstand beside the bed and onto the floor. I felt Liv beside me. Her body stirred and came alive as well.

"I told you to put that phone on silent..." Liv said.

Ignoring her, I glanced at the screen and saw that the caller was my mother. A strange sense of foreboding washed over me. It was a little past two in the morning. "Hello?"

"Sean..." my mother said before losing her voice to sobs.

That woke me all the way up instantly. I sat straight up in the bed. "Ma? Ma, what's wrong? Fuck you crying for?"

"Shontay... Shontay..."

"Shontay what, Ma? Is something wrong with Shontay?"

"She's dead! Somebody killed my baby..."

My heart heard my mother before my brain could fully discern the words I'd heard as it broke apart. Once my brain registered my mother's words, tears filled my eyes. My chest constricted and I couldn't breathe. "What?"

"Somebody shot Shontay by her car. They killed her!"

I couldn't hear anything after the word killed. I dropped the phone from my hand. My body was still, unmoving.

"Sean... baby... what happened to Shontay?" Liv asked, her body in a sitting position next to mine. When I didn't answer, Liv reached for my cell phone and put it to her ear. "Mrs. Branch, what happened to Shontay?"

"My daughter is dead," I repeated to myself. "Somebody killed her." Once I heard my own voice in my ears, I could move again. I got out of the bed and stood up.

"Sean, where are you...?"

My knees buckled and I dropped to the floor. A sound that started deep inside of me escaped my mouth. I couldn't recognize it. It was a mix between a scream and a howl. Then Liv was beside me. Her arms around my neck, her face near mine. I could hear her cries and feel her tears. Someone had told me once that our children were born into the world connected to us by spirit and blood. When one side died, the connection of spirit and blood was broken only to be connected again when both sides died. Deep inside I could feel the disconnect. I could feel the loss of my daughter's blood, her energy, her connection to me. The feeling was indescribable but there, nonetheless. I rose from my position on the floor, Liv trying to cling to me. Easily, I shook her from our embrace and wordlessly looked for my clothes. I found the outfit that I'd worn the day before near the entrance to the bedroom. The clothes lay in a heap where I'd discarded them hours ago as I attacked Liv passionately. I began to dress.

"Sean... where are you going?" Liv asked.

I didn't respond, just continued to get dressed.

Liv tried to grab me, to hold me. "Sean, baby..."

Gently, I pushed Liv away from me. I found two of my guns on her dresser. I grabbed them and put them both on my waist.

"Sean, please don't leave. Let me help ya! We can get..."

I turned and left the room. I could hear Liv's pleas to me as she followed me to the front door. Grabbing my coat out of the closet near the door, I never said a word to her. I was past the point of listening. I was past the point of talking. All I wanted to do was kill.

***

620 Evarts Street NE
"I hope you're satisfied."

I leaned on the wall of the living room with my head bowed as I listened to my mother talk. I lifted my head to see her. It seemed like my mother had aged twenty years in a matter of hours. Her salt and pepper wavy ponytail seemed to be all gray. The line in her sixty-year-old face was more pronounced. Her eyes appeared hollow. "Why would you say something like that?"

"Because, it's all I can think of. You have been in these streets hurting people and killing people for as long as I can remember. As much as I loved Ameen Bashir, I curse the decision I made to bring him into this house. You've always had your father's temper and his blood runs cold in your veins, but it was Ameen who turned you into this thing that you are today. And the thing that you are — the pain and sorrow that you've dished out to too many families to count is now back here. Right on our doorstep. The chickens coming home to roost. Shontay was innocent in this. That baby had nothing to do with what you did in them streets, but tonight she paid for it... paid for *your* sins with her life. You know it and I know it. That damn girl didn't have any enemies. All she did was work and spend too much damn time on that social media shit. She mourned her mother's death still. Everyday. In silence. Ignoring all the whispers that it was you... the father that she loved with all her heart, who killed her mother. And even as I held that girl and comforted her, told her that an insane, mad person did all that sick shit to her mom, deep inside I knew that the insane person was you.

"I remember years ago when I visited you in USP Florence, you told me that you was going to kill Raquel. You vented about her betraying you and abandoning you and having other men around your daughter. I have only seen you cry once since your daddy died. So, when I saw the tears in your eyes on that visit years ago, I knew that you would do exactly as you said you would and kill that girl. I cried because of the sickness that you have. The desire to kill and destroy. The bible says that the devil only comes to kill, steal and destroy. So, you know what that makes you, right? The fucking devil, and there you stand with your big Muslim beard and a chain around your neck that bears a silver medallion of Arabic letters that spell Allah. In Islam Allah means God, right? How can the devil wear jewelry that says God on it? How can the devil say prayers to God? Then, as soon as you finish praying, you do exactly what God hates. You kill! You steal souls! You destroy families!" My mother fell into a fit of screams, cries and shakes. She started talking to herself and shaking her head. My mother collapsed to the floor. "I hope you're satisfied, devil. I hope you're satisfied."

I rushed to my mother's fallen body and carefully helped her up from the floor. She collapsed into me and cried her heart out. I cried just as hard as her. Then suddenly, my mother started to fight me. Her fist pummeled against me. I held her tighter to reduce the force of her punches.

"Get off me, devil! This is all your fault! They killed her because of you! Take your dirty hands off of me." With a mighty burst of strength, my mother pushed away from me.

I stumbled back a few feet. My eyes went instantly to the gun in my mother's hand. I felt my waist and the empty space where the gun had just been seconds ago spoke to me. I steadied myself for whatever came next. I welcomed death.

"Do it, ma! Go ahead and end my misery! End my pain! Kill me! Do it!" I bellowed, spit flying from my mouth. "Living without my daughter will never be living again! I'd rather die! Kill me!"

To my surprise, my mother laughed. A loud thunderous cackle. She looked me straight in the eyes.; her tears falling steadily. "Who said anything about killing you? You're the devil and only God can kill you. I want you to go on living. I want you to live knowing that you caused two deaths tonight..."

Confusion etched across my face. "Two deaths? What..."

"You heard me right. You caused two deaths tonight. Shontay's and mine." My mother put the barrel of the gun in her mouth and pulled the trigger.

"N-O-O-O-O-O-O-O-!"

Everything that happened next moved in slow motion. The back of my mother's head exploded into a mist of blood and brain matter, coating the couch behind her. Her body dropped where it stood, her head bouncing as it hit the floor. A pool of blood instantly coated the carpet under her. The gun was still in her hand. I tried to scream again, but nothing came out my mouth. My mother's eyes were open and stared at something that only she could see in death. I walked over to her fallen body and dropped to my knees. Laying my head and arms on her chest that was devoid of life, I cried like a baby.

Chapter 3

Greg Gamble
Lafayette Square Park
1600 Pennsylvania Avenue
Washington, DC

"It's ironic that you asked to meet here, Sal," I said as soon as the middle-aged white man sat down next to me on the bench. I broke off the edges of bread on my sandwich and tossed them into the grass near my feet.

He looked at me directly. Salvatori Levin never looked at me directly. He sat his briefcase down on the ground at his feet and stared straight ahead at the White House grounds surrounded by a fortified black gate and secret service policeman. "How so, Greg?"

"Because the man who controls the country's lives in that house over there and he's the first black man to do so. He's a powerful man, Sal. Handsome as hell, too."

Sal Levin laughed.

"Did you know that I was the youngest man to become U.S. Attorney for the District of Columbia?"

"The first black man to hold the office, I know, but the youngest man to be U.S. Attorney, no. Didn't know that, Greg."

"As we speak, there are forces at work to bring that man down over there. There are people who live to unseat the former senator from Chicago. They question his citizenship. His religion. His allegiance to this country. I often wonder about legacy. His and mine." I reached into my coat and pulled out a manilla envelope. I passed the envelope to Sal. "Inside that envelope, you have everything you need to humble Margerie Roth, Susan Rosenthal and the great Carlos Trinidad."

"Carlos Trinidad?"

I nodded. "You're probably wondering what the Latin drug kingpin has to do with any of this, right?"

"Add mind-reader to your long list of skills."

"Carlos Trinidad is the linchpin that holds Marg Ros, and Susan together. Susan Rosenthal has been in an intimate relationship with Trinidad for almost two decades. The world believes that Gannet Communications, the company that employs Marg Ros, is owned by Kyle Hurst, but that's a lie. Gannet is owned by Venegas Enterprises..."

"I've heard a lot about Venegas Enterprises. The company is heavy into commercial real estate. They're a venture capital corporation recently gone public on the New York stock exchange. Nasdaq ranks Venegas..."

"As one of the most powerful companies in the U.S., I know. But what you don't know, what the world doesn't know, is that Venegas Enterprises is owned and operated by Carlos Trinidad."

"Have you lost your senses, Gamble? There's no way that..."

I cut Sal off. "It's in the envelope, Sal. everything you need. Check it out. Carlos Trinidad wasn't born Carlos Trinidad. He was born Carlos Venegas. He was raised here in DC by a man named Julio Trinidad. After Trinidad was murdered in his home, along with several of his gang, a young Carlos avenged his death and then took his surname as his own. Carlos Venegas became Carlos Trinidad. Venegas Enterprises is Trinidad's brainchild. The company was established in 1991 and funded by the proceeds of drug money. Margerie Roth's father, Martin Roth's birth name is Martine Rothchild. A descendant of those Rothchilds. He partnered with men associated with the cartels and was introduced to Trinidad. Martin Roth created Venegas Enterprises. When he went into retirement, he put Marg Roth in position to run Gannet surreptitiously. She pretends to be an employee, but in reality, she's the de facto CEO. But Carlos Trinidad chairs the board behind the scenes and calls all the shots. Margerie Roth has also been in an intimate relationship with Carlos Trinidad for years."

"But... Margerie Roth is married to William Weiss..."

"Sal, Malinda Gates is married to Bill and he's one of the richest men in the world, but she's been caught cheating with her yoga instructor. Marg Roth can be so lucky. Anyway, everything you need is there in that envelope. When I give you the word or if anything should ever happen to me..."

"Greg, you're giving me the creeps here. Gosh! You're being cryptic and paranoid..."

"Sometimes, paranoia is good, Sal. I have to get to work. I'll be in touch soon."

***

United States Attorney's Office
555 4th St. NW
Conference Room
"An innocent bystander was fatally shot Thursday outside of a string of shops in Northwest Shaw neighborhood. Gunfire erupted during a dispute involving three men. Apparently there was a physical altercation that ensued after an argument in the vestibule of a food shop. It spilled onto the sidewalk where one of the three men produced a handgun and opened fire." Ian McNeely reported. "A police officer happened to be near the scene and ran to the sound of gunshots. A twenty-two-year-old man named Montez Carr was taken into custody and a firearm was recovered from the scene. The victim of the shooting was not one of the three men involved in the altercation at the food shop. The victim,

a woman in her early thirties named Carsonae Duffy, was struck in the upper body and rushed to Howard University Hospital where she later died. There's video footage of the entire incident. The footage shows Montez Carr with the firearm in his hand."

"Sounds like an open and shut case to me." Susan Rosenthal chimed in.

"Shouldn't be hard to indict on second degree murder," I announced. "We'll offer him a pre indictment plea to involuntary manslaughter, six to ten years. If he waits until after he's indicted, the cop becomes voluntary manslaughter, ten to fifteen years. If he goes to trial, he loses on second degree murder, we go for the max and all the bells and whistles for the gun offenses."

"He's a convicted felon as well," Ian added. "Did two years in the BOP for a previous gun conviction."

"That's even better. All the numbers go up in a few years. Give it a while before contacting his lawyer and make sure that Montez Carr knows he's up Shitt's Creek without a paddle. Next."

"Four people were shot and wounded in the last few days in each quadrant of the city," Tabitha Kearney spoke up. "In Congress Heights, Trinidad in northeast, Columbia Heights and near the Southwest waterfront. So far, all the victims are still alive and only one arrest has been made. The one arrested is a juvenile."

"Okay. We'll deal with those as all the info comes in."

"Navarro 'Tony' Hammond was ordered release by a federal judge yesterday evening," Tomas Muniz said, "and we all know what that means."

I stopped writing on my notepad. "It means that another vicious killer has been released into our communities, that's all. Lately, there's been an influx of notorious killers released from prison. Sean Branch, Antone White, Antwan Thomas, Cinquan Blakeney, Gregory Wright, Jovan James, James Carpenter, Vincent Petty, Kevin Varner, David Wilson,

Kevin Clayborne, Antonio Jones — and the list goes on and on. There's no way we can stop the floodgates from being opened and killers being released with all the new laws being passed, designed to free them. All we can do is wait until they reoffend and do our best to lock their asses back up. What else is new?"

***

"The Michael Carter hearing is in a couple days."

I looked at the open door to my office and the woman who'd just walked into it. "Did you forget how to knock on doors before you enter offices, Susan?"

Susan Rosenthal smiled. "Oh, come on, Greg. Pompous Asshole Day is today, huh? How many times have you barged into my office without knocking? What's got your panties in a bunch?"

"Disloyalty. Besides, I already know when Carter's hearing is. Me and the entire city knows about it since it's been on every news cycle for the last three or four days."

"So, that's what's got you in a foul mood. And did you say disloyalty?"

"I did."

"Who's been disloyal to you, Greg?"

"Do you listen to RNB, Susan?"

"When I can, why?"

"Because Chris Brown has a new song out called '*Loyal*.' I happen to agree with him, that's all."

"Chris Brown? You like his new song, huh? Was that before or after you played hardball with him and sent him to DC jail for assault? And why would anyone listen to Chris Brown from Tappahannock, Virginia when he beats women? Even the ones who are loyal."

"I'm just glad to know that you listen to a genre of music widely held dear by a majority of blacks. Being as though you have a predilection of the browner persuasion — I mean

Latino dick — no men, I thought all you listened to was Salsa music."

"Ain't that a racist comment, boss? Or is it chic to throw around words like that knowing that you have the backing of the LGBT community? And who do you listen to these days, Greg? Village People? Queen, the rock band? Prince? Michael Jacko?"

I laughed at Susan's attempt at witticism and sarcasm. "What do you want, Susan? Besides my job?"

"I was just wondering about your defense at the Carter hearing. Thought you'd might want to strategize a little. That's all."

"No, thank you..." I was interrupted by the intercom on my phone. I hit the button and said, "Yes, Patty?"

"Detective Robert Mathis is here. Says he needs to speak to you. It's important," Patty the receptionist said.

"Send him in," I said. To Susan Rosenthal, I said, "We'll have plenty of time to strategize about other cases. I'm good on this one."

"Are you?" Susan replied with a smile as she turned and left the office.

"Stupid bitch." I muttered to myself and laughed. "Those who laugh last laugh longer."

Seconds later, Detective Bob Mathis swept into my office. I stood up and walked around my desk. After shaking hands with the homicide detective, I said, "What's important, Bob?"

"Last night someone killed Sean Branch's daughter in a parking garage near Gallery Place. This morning, officers found Sean Branch's mother dead in her home. The streets of DC are about to be flooded with blood. Just wanted you to know that before the killing started."

Deflated, I sat on my desk and inhaled loudly. I exhaled. "Tell me everything you know."

Chapter 4
Quran

I spotted Sean's Porsche parked in the Walmart underground parking garage and headed towards it. I could still hear his words in my ear on the phone minutes ago...

"I need to holla at you, youngin. It's all bad."

Sean hung up immediately after telling me to come to the Walmart on H Street in Northeast. As I found a spot to pull into and park, I saw Sean exit the Porsche in all-black attire. Something was missing in him, I could see, but I couldn't say what it was. I backed into a space next to a Honda Accord and the wall, then hopped out of my new truck, an Infiniti QX50. I approached Sean as he leaned on the hood of the Porsche. As soon as he looked up at me I knew exactly what was missing. Sean's ever-present smile when he saw me, and his beard. On his head was a black True Religion wool cap that he pulled down over his ears. His Eddie Bauer Parka with the fur lined hood was open to reveal a black Solbiato hooded sweatshirt and an ARP attached to a string that hung from Sean's neck. A handgun protruded from the waist of his black jeans. Another handgun's butt was visible coming from Sean's jean's pocket. His eyes were bloodshot red.

"Ock, what the fuck is up with you? Why did ya cut your beard?" I asked once I was within a foot of Sean.

Sean's cold eyes stared straight through me. Tears formed in his eyes and fell down his cheeks. "Fuck that beard, youngin. My beard symbolized my Islam, but all of that's gone..."

"Gone? What's gone? The beard, I see, but the Islam? You can't be serious, and why are you crying, slim? Fuck is up?"

"For years..." Sean wiped at the tears on his face. "For years, all I had to keep me sane was Allah, Islam, my mother and my daughter. The four of them got me through all the rough times in prison. Helped me to remain human. Today, I lost it all, youngin. Everything. There's no buffer between me and the animal inside me. Today, I'm a different man. A changed man."

"Ock, you're confusing me. I'm lost. How have you changed? Other than your appearance without the beard? And what did you lose today? What do you mean by everything? You lost everything?"

The tears in Sean's eyes were determined to fall, and after a while he let them fall without wiping them. Sean was silent for what seemed like an eternity. Suddenly, he screamed out loud. I looked around the parking garage to see what and whose attention he'd drawn, but the garage was deserted.

"I'ma kill everybody — nobody is safe — I swear to God!"

I stood transfixed to my spot and watched my partner, my brother, my mentor totally come unglued. Sean swung combinations in the air as he cried. Spit flew from his mouth as he cursed and gyrated. Punched the air and dropped to his knees. Sean laid on the ground and covered his head as he cried loudly. He kicked his feet and squirmed on the ground as if being electrocuted by currents that only he could feel. I couldn't believe my eyes. I was dumbstruck. I was confused. I was afraid. I dropped to one knee to try and pick Sean up from the ground, but he snatched away from my grasp. One of the guns in his pocket or waist hit the ground with a loud sound. Metal against concrete. I stood up and just watched as Sean went through a fit of every kind of emotion. He cried loudly, then softly. He talked to himself. He swore. He kicked and punched the ground. He turned over onto his back and uncovered his face. The grief on his face was palpable. I only glimpsed at it for a quick second before he covered his face and cried like a petulant child throwing a fit. I didn't know what to do or what to say. So, I did nothing and said nothing. A man with a shopping cart and a toddler in tow appeared out of nowhere. He looked down at Sean then up at me. He said no words. Just grabbed at the hand of the kid and kept it moving.

"Bruh... we gotta go." I called out to Sean. "You making a scene. Someone's gonna call the cops. Get up! Let's go!"

As if my words were the magic elixir that he needed, Sean did as I said. He slowly rose from the ground and brushed himself off. He reached down and picked up the gun that had fallen. Then without a backward glance, Sean walked over to my truck and got into the passenger seat.

***

I drove around the city aimlessly with no particular destination in mind. Occasionally, I'd glance over at Sean who sat quiet in the front passenger seat with the seat reclined as far as it would go. His hat now covered his eyes. All I could do was watch the ARP on the string around his neck rise and fall with every breath he took. Sean hadn't said one word since I'd left the Walmart parking garage. I'd been around Sean long enough to understand that he'd talk only once he was good and ready. He couldn't be prodded, he wasn't to be pressured. So, I drove. Drove and thought about what little Sean had said to me before his breakdown in the garage.

"For years — for years, all I had to keep me sane was Allah, Islam, my mother and my daughter. The four of them got me through all the rough times in prison. Helped me to remain human. Today, I lost it all, youngin. Everything. There's no buffer between me and the animal inside me..."

"Today, I'm a different man. A changed man," I said aloud, remembering Sean's every word, wondering what they meant. As fate would have it, I didn't have to wonder long.

Hearing the words I spoke must have awakened Sean and roust him from a dark place; a coma of some kind. "You're a good listener, Que. Another reason why I really fuck with you." Sean didn't move. He never lifted the wool cap from his eyes, he just started talking. "You heard me say that I'm different now. That I have changed. I meant every word I said. You just witnessed the evolution of Sean Branch. I've evolved. I was half man, half animal before. Now, I'm all animal. I will never cry again after today. Never hurt. Never be compassionate and never stop halfway through total annihilation. You think I was crazy before. Wait until you witness the new me. I was against ops and rats before. And anyone who stoked my ire. Now, anybody can get it. *Anybody!*"

"Damn, Ock! I don't like the way that sounds. What happened to make you feel like this? Why the sudden evolution?"

"Life happened, Que. Life happened. And I ain't gon lie, youngin. This is the hardest blow I've ever taken. Since my father got killed in prison. Since your father got killed."

"Earlier, you said that today you lost everything."

"I did. Last night, somebody killed my daughter after she got off work..."

"Hell naw!" I shouted.

"Hell, yeah." Sean replied calmly. "Shot her multiple times by her car in a parking garage near the Chipotle where she worked. The cops— this detective named Mathis contacted my mother— went to her house and told her all about it. They call it notifying the next of kin. My mother IDed Shontay from pictures on his phone. My mother called me to tell me. I go to the house in Langdon Park and saw my mother in mourning. She told me everything the cop said.

29

Then she blames me for Shontay's death. Asked me was I satisfied that I'd finally lost everything. Before I could answer— before I could say a word— she killed herself."

"Bruh— no! I'm sorry..."

"No need to be sorry, youngin'. All of this is my fault. Mines and Allah. I believed in Allah and trusted Allah to keep my family safe. I made dua... I prayed all the time and begged Allah to punish me, but to keep my daughter and mother out of what I did in the streets. I kinda thought that we had that understanding, slim. I thought that Allah had heard my prayers and answered them, too. This incident— these incidents— have shown me that either Allan didn't hear my supplications, He did hear them and ignored them, or lastly, He just doesn't exist. Considering what I've been through in the last twelve hours, I've decided to focus on the latter. There is no higher power — no creator, no omnipotent, omnipresent, ubiquitous being above or around us. The idea of Allah died with my daughter and mother. Without Allah, there is no Islam. No Islam, no beard. There's nothing but me, these guns and vengeance. In the bible, it says that vengeance is mine sayeth the Lord. Well, I *am* the Lord and I declare that *vengeance is mine*, and everybody who comes to mind as a suspect in my daughter's murder will die."

I pulled the Infiniti truck over to the curb somewhere near the 14th Street bridge. "Big bruh, I understand where your mind is at. I get it, really I do, but you trippin'. You can't let go of the rope of Allah. It's all we have..."

"It's all *you* have, Que. Me, not so much. Not anymore. Religion has no place in my life anymore. Prayer and fasting and Jumah has no place in the jungle where the animals roam. I am the animal that lives in a jingle. And the jungle creed is that either you kill or be killed. And I'm determined to do as much killing as I can before I'm killed. You cannot convince me to change my mind, Que. I am not the person that you knew from 24 hours ago. It is what it is. Figured that I'd let you be the first to hear me. To know my reality. My truth." Sean lifted the wool cap from his eyes, leaned forward and looked out the window of the truck. "I'm about to turn up, youngin, and where I'm headed, you don't need to be. If I was able to love, this is the part where I'd tell you that I love you, but that part of me is gone. Taken away with the lives of my daughter and mother. Shit is about to get real wicked. I hope that our paths never have to cross in a bad way. I'ma get out right here. Take care, youngin'." And with that said, Sean Branch exited the truck and walked away.

***

"Somebody killed Sean's daughter last night."

"What?" Zin exclaimed. "No!"

I paced the floor in Zin's office as I thought about everything that Sean had said to me earlier. I nodded my head. "Yeah. And that's not all. His mother was notified as next of kin. She told Sean. He went to her house. Sean's mother blamed his daughter's murder on him, then she killed herself..."

Zin rose from her chair, her face a mask of disbelief. "No way. Are you sure?"

"Sean called me. Met me earlier. Told me everything. His mother took a gun from his waist as he hugged her. Before he could stop her, she put the gun in her mouth and committed suicide. Right there in front of Sean."

"Oh... My... Gawd!"

"Sean's fucked up, baby. He's lost all control. Says he's about to turn up. He's gonna kill until he can't kill anymore and then... and then..."

Zin rushed to me and hugged me. "Quran, I'm sorry, baby. I know how close you and Sean are. I'm sorry about Sean's daughter and his mother, but that's Sean's situation. It's his cross he has to bear. Not yours. I need you, Quran. Our baby needs you. Jihad needs you. Please don't partner yourself with Sean and go down the road he's going down. Please...

don't do that. Sean Branch is a killer, Quran. A cold-blooded killer whose been killing people for decades. Whatever he's done recently or in his past has brought despair, pain and death to his front door, just like he's done to countless others. He's not you! What he eats doesn't make you shit! Don't go off on a killing spree with Sean, Que. That road leads only to jail or Harmony Cemetery. Stay focused for me, baby!"

I put my arms around Zin and squeezed her tight. "I'm focused. Sean didn't ask me to partner with him. In fact, he cut me off and lightweight threatened me."

"Threatened you? Threatened you for what?"

"For reasons known to only him, he told me that he hoped our paths never crossed in a bad way. He said that right before he hopped out the truck and bounced. He told me that where he's headed, I didn't need to be."

"And he was right, baby. He was so fuckin' right to tell you that. The shit he's about to be on ain't for you. He's focused on the dead— the ones he's lost and the ones he's about to kill. You have to focus on the living. Your life, my life, your unborn child's life, and Jihad's life. Anything other than that doesn't matter, baby. Do you agree?"

"I agree, Zin. I agree."

"Good," Zin said and let me go. "Go and lock my office door."

"Lock your office door?" I repeated. "Why?"

"Duh? So that you can fuck me without interruption. Damiyah might walk in here if the door is open or unlocked. You got me a little stressed all of a sudden. I need to relieve that stress."

Smiling and shaking my head, I did as I was told. I locked Zin's office door. When I turned back around, Zin's skirt was on the floor in a pile with her blouse and heels. Dressed in only her panties and matching bra, Zin sat down in the chair in front of her desk. She threw one leg up onto the chair's arm. I looked down at the platinum anklet that encircled Zin's ankle and the silver polish that covered her toenails.

That was enough to arouse me totally. Walking over to where Zin sat in the chair, I dropped to my knees. I pulled her panties down and then lifted her other leg to the other arm of the chair. Zin's pussy had a light landing strip of pubic hair above the clit. I focused on it as I kissed her there, then made my way down. At Zin's clit, I found perfection. I found love. I gave her love and affection. I gave Zin ecstasy.

***

"Quran, I'm serious about what I said earlier. You got enough shit on your plate already. Don't add Sean's shit to it."

I sat in the chair that I had just sexed Zin in and leaned back in it. My eyes were closed but my ears were open.

"I hate to beat a dead horse, but I can't forget about all that shit that Nikki told me the other day. About all the investigations you're a part of. Is there any evidence that connects you to your brother's murder? Thomas Caldwell or Yolonda Stevens?"

"If there was any evidence and they had it, I'd be in jail already, don't you think?"

"Yeah, but what about the Maryland case?"

"I already told you, baby, that I was probably one of the last people to see her or talk to Tosheka before she was killed. Who knows what they have. But one thing is for sure, if Maryland had anything, I'd be in jail out in upper Marlboro. They're fishing. I didn't kill Tosheka, so they can investigate all they want. My DNA or fingerprints in her apartment can be explained. I had no reason to kill that woman."

"What about Jihad and David?"

"What about them?" I asked.

"Do you trust them?" Zin replied.

"You already know the answer to that question."

"I asked you did you trust David after I learned that Greg Gamble talked to him in the infirmary at the jail. You said you trusted him. But times have changed. Circumstances are different now. The stakes are higher with the focus now being on you for several murders. You and Jihad both said y'all trusted David. I'ma ask you again and I need a straight answer. Do you trust David Battle?"

"I trust Dave, yeah. I trust him."

"Your brother Khitab was raised by you. You believed that he'd never tell on anyone. You were wrong. Do you trust Jihad?"

I opened my eyes and leaned forward. I spun the chair around to face Zin who was now sitting behind her desk, fully clothed. "I trust Jihad with my life. He will never betray me. He'd rather die than cross me."

"I sure hope so, Quran. I really hope that's true. For all of our sake."

Chapter 5
Michael Carter

"Last night, a twenty-year-old woman was killed after leaving work at a Chipotle in Northwest. The victim was identified as Shontay Rokia Dunn. Ms. Dunn was shot multiple times in the face and body. Local authorities are still investigating this tragedy. CUS Fox News have just learned that this story gets worse. Standard operating procedure for law enforcement is to notify the next of kin after a victim of violent crime dies. A homicide detective went to the home of Shontay Dunn to notify her of her relative's death. After hearing a single gunshot hours later, neighbors of that relative called police. A wellness check was ordered after police received no reply from inside the home. Police entered the residence forcefully and discovered a woman, the woman who'd been notified about her granddaughter's murder, dead from a self-inflicted gunshot wound. That woman has been identified as 55-year-old Sharon Branch..."

"What the fuck?" I said to myself as I got up from the table inside the TV room in my unit. I walked out of the TV room and descended the steps quickly. I was inside my cell in seconds. I sat down on the bottom bunk and thought about what I'd just heard on the news. Shontay Dunn was Sean Branch's daughter and Sharon Branch was his mother. "Man, what the fuck is going on out there?" I got up from the bunk and dropped to the floor. I did a set of fifty pushups, rested for a few seconds and then repeated the rep. Standing up, I leaned on the cell wall and held back tears. No matter how I felt about Sean nowadays, I never wished death on his family.

Memories of Sharon Branch came to mind. The woman was one of the baddest chicks in Northeast in her prime. Her exotic good looks and dark curly hair made her the envy of a lot of women in D.C. in the eighties and nineties. At a young age, Sharon had gone off and married Bruno Branch, a notorious criminal from her neighborhood. From their union, they produced one son. Sean. Bruno Branch was arrested for a double murder and sentenced to a rack of time in the Maryland Correctional system. Not long after arriving at the notorious Cut Annex Maximum security prison, Bruno was stabbed and killed. If her husband's death was a blow to Sharon, she hid it well. Months later, Sharon hooked up with Ameen Bashir and they became a couple. I remember all the times I'd envied Ameen silently as I saw him and Sharon together.

After Ameen's death, Sharon Branch had needed comforting. I stepped in to do the job. I fucked Sharon a few times, but declared her used goods with a real mental problem. I eased away from Sharon and focused on her son. Ameen Bashir had groomed Sean to kill by the time he was eleven or twelve. By the time Sean was fourteen, his reputation as a killer was solidified. After Ameen's death, Sean Branch was mine to mold, to train, to direct. I could also remember the young woman that Sean loved with all his heart. Raquel Dunn. A fair haired, caramel complexion stunner that everybody wanted. I remember when Raquel was pregnant with Sean's first child, his only child. Raquel had a daughter and named her Shontay after her father. I leaned on the wall in my cell and remembered going to the hospital after the baby was born. I'd taken gifts and balloons. I'd seen the baby girl and instantly was reminded of Zin. The baby girl was the spitting image of her father. Over the next year or so, I'd seen Shontay a couple times with Sean. He doted on that little girl. She was the light that twinkled in his dark eyes. And now she was gone. Killed seven months after her father's release from prison. Seven months that I had not heard one word from Sean. What the hell had he done to make someone kill his daughter?

I shook my head as I remembered what the news said. Sharon Branch had taken her own life after learning that her granddaughter was murdered. *Damn!* What a tragic end to an urban saga.

"It's not the end," I said to myself. "It's not over."

Couldn't be over. Because as sure as flies were attracted to shit, Sean Branch was about to take his grief out on the entire city.

***

"You got a pass, Carter," the CO inside the bubble said after motioning for me to come over. "Here. Go to the first floor. The pass is for the chapel. The chaplain called for you."

The chaplain called for me? Immediately, I thought about Zin and my sister Linda. I walked away from the bubble in a daze. If something had happened to either of the women I loved with all my heart, I didn't know what I'd do. As I walked into my cell and prepared to see the chaplain, all types of things came to mind. All kinds of wild scenarios. Sean and Quran beefing. Sean had hurt Zin, and Quran avenged her by killing Shontay and Sharon. I shook all those thoughts from my mind as I brushed my teeth.

***

"Michael Carter?" Chaplain Green asked as soon as I entered the area designated as the chapel at the DC jail. The mature black woman was an exact replica of Pam Grier.

I nodded. "Yes, ma'am that's me."

"Probably thought I called you here to give you news about a loved one dying or something, right?"

"Kinda sorta."

"Well, fortunately, this is not that type of visit today. I have you scheduled to see the priest today..."

"Priest? What priest?" I asked, befuddled.

"Just have a seat and Father Lopez will be in to see you momentarily. Go sit in the chair in front of my desk."

I hadn't asked to see no priest. I wasn't even Catholic. I did as instructed by Chaplain Green.

Minutes later, a man walked into the office. A Hispanic man dressed in the clerical vestiges of a priest. Once the man turned to face me completely, I recognized him instantly. "Carlos?"

Carlos Trinidad grabbed a vacant chair and sat it directly across from me. He sat in the chair that was literally only a foot or two away. He smiled. "It's been, what... twenty years, Mike, since we last saw one another?"

"Not quite twenty... well, maybe twenty. What a surprise."

"Surprise is my middle name, Mike, haven't you heard? But enough chit chat, let me get right to the point of my visit. After you've had your evidentiary hearing, you're going to be a free man. And although I believe in redemption and justice, I haven't decided whether or not you get to live, Mike. I haven't decided whether or not Linda Carter gets to live or even your daughter Zinfandel, the defense lawyer. What I hear from you today will help me to make those decisions, Mike. So, please, think before you speak. I hope that what I've said hasn't disturbed you or unsettled you. What I'm about to say is fact. Plain and simple fact. I know in 1995 that you didn't kill Dontay Samuels. I knew that Ameen's son, Quran, killed him. I knew that Greg Gamble was framing you for that murder and I also knew why he was doing it. At any time, Mike, I could have put an end to the charade. I could have stepped in and saved the day for you before and after that jury of your peers found you guilty of a murder that you didn't commit. But I didn't. I chose not to help you. When you went to Lorton, Mike, I could've had you killed instantly. When you were transferred to federal prison in 2001, the act of having you killed became even more easier. Your simple scheme — your murder for hire scheme that you've been running from prison for years was all my idea and you never even knew it. I know all about the murders that Ameen Bashir's sons have been committing for you. I know everything. But what I don't know— what I'm here to find out— is why you killed Ameen Bashir. I loved Ameen. He was a valued person to me and to my organization. I always suspected that it was you who killed him, but I wasn't sure. Now, I'm sure that it was you. I want to know why you did it. And be careful what you say, Mike. Choose your words wisely because the lives of your family also hangs in the balance. You've witnessed firsthand my brand of justice. I'd hate to ruin everything you've built, what your daughter has built, because of deceit and arrogance." Carlos moved his chair closer. "So, please, tell me why you killed Ameen Bashir?"

I never imagined that a day like this would come. I always played the game fair with Carlos Trinidad and unbeknownst to him, he'd just confirmed something that I had always suspected but could never confirm. Ameen had known Carlos Trinidad *before* our first meeting at Dela Rosa's in Columbia Road all those years ago. Then, inadvertently, Carlos had confirmed certain irrefutable truths for me. Had he forgotten that? My confidence waned and my composure slagged a little before the powerful drug lord, but I stiffened my resolve and decided that I would never completely cower in the face of death or a stronger opponent, or adversary. "If you cross me once, you'll cross me twice. Remember that, Carlos?"

"How could I ever forget it? It was something I learned from my uncle Julio. I kept his memory alive every time I passed that saying on. What about it?"

"Ameen betrayed me, Carlos. He crossed me to be with my wife."

To my surprise, Carlos Trinidad laughed. "Mike, do you realize just how powerful I really am?"

"You're sitting in front of me inside of the DC jail, dressed as a priest. I think that says how truly powerful you must be."

"In the position that I'm in, my greatest asset is information. Information is power, Mike. I knew all about Ameen's affair with your wife, Patricia. I also know that before Ameen slept with your wife, you slept with his. You had an affair with Khadijah Bashir *before* Ameen got with Patricia. So, it's you who crossed Ameen first. Her youngest child is rumored to be— *was* rumored to be— your child. Ameen never knew that. It was you who betrayed him first."

"I accept that, Carlos, but it's not true. *Ameen* crossed me first. Ameen knew Patricia, had sexed Patricia *before* Patricia and I met. Ameen broke Patricia in, when she was twelve years old. I met her as a fourteen-year-old. Ameen was with me the day we met, but yet he said nothing about his relationship with Patricia. Maybe he was ashamed of the fact that his actions were a little pedophilic because he was seven or eight years her senior when their sex began. Maybe that's why he never told me initially, but where was his loyalty to me when he continued to have sex with Patricia then and after her pregnancy and our eventual marriage? I was crossed first by Ameen then and later! Before Ameen's death, I met with you..."

"At one of my establishments in Georgetown. I remember that."

"Well, that day you and I talked about several things. But you inadvertently said to me more than I believe you meant to say. I left that conversation, that meeting with several confirmations. I had grown to suspect Ameen's betrayal days before but wasn't sure about what I suspected. You gave me the answers I needed."

"What answers?"

"When I was summoned by you to attend our first ever sit down at DelaRosa's, Ameen acted as if he was surprised by the summons and never told me that he knew you. Did business with you. Why? Ameen used to say your saying, Carlos. The first time I'd ever heard, 'If you cross me once, you'll cross me twice,' I heard that from Ameen. But it never dawned on me that he'd gotten that from you until *after* I found him with Patricia, in our bed the night I flew with you to the Catskills. The night you murdered Victor Martinez's family. After you and I talked at that meeting in Georgetown, I left knowing that Ameen had taken hits for you for your organization and that it was Ameen who had suggested two things to you about me. Ameen suggested that you'd get me to kill Victor Martinez and let me take over his territory and position selling cocaine. And it was also Ameen who suggested that you take me to New York when you went there to eradicate Victor Martinez's bloodline. He told you that it would be good for me to witness your brand of street justice firsthand and that it would keep me loyal and in line. I learned then that Ameen orchestrated the events of that evening. He manipulated us both, Carlos. Why? Just so that he could spend an uninterrupted night with my wife. But what Ameen didn't anticipate was that I'd come home that night after I'd already told him that I wouldn't return until the next day. I returned that night and saw Ameen in the bed making love to my wife and it broke me. Your words wouldn't leave my head..."

"And please, Mike, never ever try to cross me. The first time I will have you killed. Why? Because if you cross me once, you'll cross me twice."

"So, knowing what I knew at the time, I made the decision to kill my best friend because he had crossed me. Not once, not twice, but several times. Does that answer your question? I killed Ameen Bashir because he crossed me. And despite the fact that you're wearing a priest outfit, you're in no position to judge me harshly, Carlos. Why? Because if you were in my position, you would have done the same thing. Would you have not?"

Carlos Trinidad's hair was salt and peppered, but dark and curly. His facial features were set into his face like chiseled stone. His teeth were perfectly aligned, his smile immaculate, yet menacing. He leaned back in his chair and steepled his hands atop his head. All the while, his dark and hooded eyes were on me. "I would have. For all the deception you've mentioned, I would have killed my best friend, too. I understand everything you've said and I feel that you have spoken truthfully. No harm will come to you or your family by my hand or words. Once you are a free man, Mike, we will talk again. And not on the telephone. I'll find you and send for you. Is there anything that you need to make your stay here at the jail more comfortable?"

"I'm good. You've done more than enough with the phone."

Carlos rose from his chair. "If you need anything, Mike, contact me and you'll have it."

"Thank you, Carlos. For listening to me."

"I owe you that much, Michael Carter. Before I leave, though, I have one more question for you."

"Shoot."

"Quran Bashir and his brother Jihad, do they know you killed their father?"

"No," I replied. "Hopefully, they'll never know that."

"Let's hope not. Take care, Mike," Carlos said and left the room.

It was at least ten minutes later after Carlos Trinidad left the room that I realized that I'd been shaking the entire time.

Chapter 6

Jihad
Central Treatment Facility
1901 E Street SE

"One of these niggas in here talking, slim."

I put down the urban novel I was reading to give Dave my undivided attention. We were out in the day room. "Why you say that?"

"Because them muthafuckas— the cops— been in my cell twice in the last three days. Then the maintenance people was in the chase closet in between my cell twice this morning. Bitches probably bugged my cell."

"Or you can just be being paranoid, big homie."

"Maybe. Maybe not. You hear that wild shit about somebody killing Sean Branch's daughter yesterday?"

"Yeah, one of my bitches told me this morning. Said it was all over the news. She said that his mother killed herself after she got the news about Sean's daughter. I know that homie is out there about to turn up."

"Did you ever meet Sean?" Dave asked.

"Once. Big bruh introduced me to him one day. He seemed cool."

"That's the shit that tricks niggas, slim. And he been tricking niggas since the early nineties, late eighties. Dangerous muthafucka. You talk to Que?"

I shook my head. "Not since I talked to him and told him all the shit that Charles Daum told me."

43

"What did he say about that shit?"

"Just that he was already hipped and that Nikki Locks had told Zin the same shit already. Let him tell it, he ain't worried about nothing."

Dave laughed. "My muthafuckin' man, Iceberg Que. Nigga got ice water running through his veins. My fuckin' main man's a fuckin' savage. Speaking of savage, did I tell you that my lil' man Antbone done caught the nigga that hit me down South One and cooked his ass?"

I reached out for my book and picked it up. "I think you told me that." I opened the book and began to read a page.

"That joint a mean joint, huh?"

"What? This book?" I replied to Dave's question.

"Yeah, the book. I been hearing about that Ultimate Sacrifice for years. Is it good?"

I nodded. "Bad muthafucka. I'm glad bruh sent me these joints. It's a trilogy."

"The dude that wrote them joints is over at the jail. Came back on a writ from the Feds. Niggas got slim name in their mouths the wrong way and homie ain't having it, I heard. See, that nigga over there," Dave said while pointing at a dude with dreads and a rack of tats. The dude had bandages on damn near seventy percent of his body. "See him?"

I nodded my head, then went back to the book. "I see him. Why, what's up with him?"

"How do you think he got the way he is?" Dave asked and smiled.

"Fuck if I know."

"The dude who wrote that book did it. The CO told me. The dude who wrote the book is named Buckey Fields. Slim over there was running his mouth about homie and had no clue that Buckey Fields was sitting a couple feet away from him at one of the tables in the day room over at the jail. Worthy told me that the homie cooked slim ass. Got the man sitting over there looking like a mummy or something. Stupid niggas. Should've kept his fuckin' mouth closed about shit he don't know nothing about. Niggas always repeating shit that they heard a nigga say, even if the shit ain't true. I bet his stupid ass'll watch his tongue next time, won't he?"

Laughing at Dave, I stood up to leave. "Big homie, you ain't gon' rap me up because you had to flush your cell phone. I'm getting ready to go get on my new joint. I'ma holla back."

"Oh, yeah, Jay? That's foul, slim. Reach out to bruh and tell him I need a new joint, ASAP. And I need to see our girl soon."

"I got you, slim. I got you."

"Aye, and one more thing. See if Que has talked to Mike Carter since he been at the jail."

"I'll ask, but I don't think so. He would've said something to me about it and he didn't. When I mentioned Mike, bruh's whole demeanor changed like Mike might be the op now. I might be wrong, though, I'ma ask him and let you know what he says."

"Damn, one more thing," Dave said and smiled.

"What, bruh? What's good?"

"You got some more weed left? If so, get me."

Chapter 7
Zin

"Ms. Carter, how do dudes like me defend ourselves in here? The new cultural phenomenon is niggas jumpin' on niggas' cases. The way the system is set up, these wild ass niggas in here can just listen to your phone conversation, shit you say on the tier, hear rumors about your case or go through your shit when you ain't in the cell. Then they get on the phone and get in contact with your prosecutor and lie on a nigga to jump on your case..."

"Don't talk on the phone. Don't talk on the tier. Don't talk about your case to anyone. Friend or family member. Just shut the fuck up..."

"Yeah, yeah, I get all that, but that still don't stop these fuckin' rats from jumpin' on niggas' cases. A man can't be at two places at once and you can't take your discovery in the shower with you. Fuck is a man supposed to do? If I'm at court or on a legal visit like right now, who's to say that my celly ain't going through my mail and shit, right now? Look what the fuck this nigga Russell Wiseman doing right now. This nigga just came back from the Feds a month ago and this nigga done jumped on three niggas from Ivy city cases already. And they young niggas, too. Them niggas were lil' kids when that nigga went to jail in 2001. He telling on some cold case murders to get back to DC and now he's the star witness on like four other cases. How the fuck can that shit be fair?"

IF YOU CROSS ME ONCE 5 | ANTHONY FIELDS

"Ima tell you the way my aunt always told me, Rashod. Fair is a festival in Ohio where they judge pies and pigs. As soon as you get the fact that this system is not designed for you, you'll understand better. A few years ago, I was teaching an after-school law class in a rec center in Northeast near Webb Elementary School."

"At Trinidad Rec Center? It's in my hood. I remember different lawyers used to come to the rec center and teach."

"Anyway, the class was getting restless when a teenage dude raised his hand. He said to me, 'I got a question. Police let drug dealers stay on the corner because they're snitching, right?' I nodded my head. The teen then asked, 'Is that legal? Can the cops really do that?' When I explained to him that the police could indeed do that and that the police have discretion to let offenders remain at large, the teen and his friends were disgusted. 'I hate the police,' one teen exclaimed suddenly. 'So, all you gotta do is snitch and you can stay out of jail and keep dealing on the corners?' asked another. Those teenagers that day received a message. A disturbing one from the criminal justice system's heavy use of snitches. They learned that day that crime is negotiable and that justice is for sale. That message is one of the great costs of the effects of the snitching phenomenon."

"I get what you're saying, Ms. Carter, but the shit is still crazy and I still gotta ask my initial question. How do dudes like me protect myself from rats who are trying to get home off of me and my men?"

I shrugged my shoulders. "All I can say is what I said. Don't talk about your case on the tier, in the block, on the court bus, in the bullpen, in your cell, on the blue wall phone, on any cell phones, to any friends or family members. Don't keep mail that mentions your case. And lastly, guard your legal papers as best you can. That's all I can tell you. Oh, and damn sure don't put nothing about your case in that novel you're writing. The feds read urban novels, too."

"Got ya, Ms. Carter. I won't. I'm not that stupid. When I finish 'The Life of A Savage', I'ma publish it under my new nickname."

"And what's that, Rashod?"

"Huff Da Great."

***

I threw up into the toilet for the second time in two minutes. Then threw up again. Being around women my entire life, I'd heard that throwing up would come with the territory of having a baby. *But wasn't it supposed to just be morning sickness?* Looking at my watch, I saw that it was almost 3PM. Definitely wasn't morning time. As I straightened up and leaned against the bathroom stall, panic set in a little. Silently, I said a prayer to God that all was well. Now that I'd gotten the idea of being a mother firmly implanted in my head and heart, I didn't want anything to change that. I wanted the baby. Quran's baby. As quickly as the queasiness in my stomach came, it left just as fast. At the sink, I freshened up and brushed my teeth. I looked in the mirror at my reflection. I looked the same and felt the same, but deep inside I was different. The last eight months had changed me. Robbed me of my innocence. Opened my eyes to the cruel and harsh realities of the world. My mother had been killed by my father for infidelity. My father had been framed for a murder he didn't commit and was incarcerated. I'd left a good, decent man in Jermaine and fell in love with a cold-blooded killer. Now I was two months pregnant by that killer. I splashed water onto my face and redid my make up. Gathering my wits, I exited the women's restroom at the DC jail. I had work to do.

***

"You didn't help your case, Mr. Williams, by assaulting Javon Jarrett."

"I should've killed his bitch ass. Excuse my language, Ms. Carter," Anthony Williams said with conviction. "He touched my old head. I had to touch him."

"Well, touching him added an AWIK to your fight to beat the murder charge you have. I understand why you did it, but I still wish you hadn't done it. The prosecutor on this case is going to have a field day portraying you as a violent young animal who happens to be black. With that being said, let's go over your case. The murder charge..."

Forty minutes later, I was preparing to leave.

"Ms. Carter, have you spoken to Dave lately?"

"I'm on my way across the street to see him in a few. Why?"

"Just give him my love and respect. Tell him that I said, 'Live The Omerta and Death before Dishonor'. He'll know what it means."

"Uh— I know what it means. I will be sure to give him the message though, Mr. Williams."

"You make me feel old, Ms. Carter. Call me Antbone."

"Have a good evening, Mr. Williams, and please stay out of trouble."

***

C.T.F.
1901 E Street SE

"So, let me get this straight, Diamond, just so we're clear. Because you screwed up and got caught with over two ounces of weed which makes your possession of marijuana into a possession with intent to distribute, a felony. And it's your third one in two years. You want me to make a deal with the government where you'll testify against your son's father on a murder he's fighting. According to you, you were on the scene when D'nell Austin was shot and killed on Lebaum

Street by Parris Knighton and Knighton's motive for killing Austin was that Knighton found out that you were sexually involved with D'nell Austin. Is that the long and short of it?"

Diamond Cantrell's eyes lit up. Her smile stretched from ear to ear with glee. The twenty-five-year-old mother of three could have been an Instagram model. She was that beautiful. "Yeah, what do you think? You think you can get me a deal like that? I tell on P-Man — that's Parris— and they'll drop my drug charge and let me go."

"Let me answer both of your questions in the order that you asked them, baby girl. Come a little closer across the table." I told the girl.

Diamond leaned closer across the table that separated us in the small legal visit room at CTF, where women prisoners in DC were held.

"Can you hear me?" I asked.

"I hear you, Ms. Carter," Diamond replied.

"I think you are a piece of shit coward for wanting to shit on your son's father like that. I don't give a fuck what kind of father he is or what he may or may not have done for you or to you. You don't get that man back like that. All you got is a bullshit distribution. At the most, you're facing three years. That's two and a half years in a sweet female facility in the feds. With a halfway house, you'd be out in two years. Two fuckin' years, Diamond. You out in the streets hustling — breaking the law. And just because you got caught slipping, you want to send Parris Knighton to prison for forty years? Real bitches do real things and it's obvious that you ain't one of them, so do what you feel you got to do. But to answer your second questions, fuck no, I can't get you no deal like that. I *wouldn't* get you no deal like that. You got the wrong attorney, boo. Tomorrow morning, I'm withdrawing from your case. We suddenly have a failure to communicate. I don't speak rat." I rose from the chair, gathered my things and left the room.

***

David Battle looked slimmer than he had when I'd last seen him. He walked into the legal visit room on the second floor with a cocksure swag. His navy two-piece CTF uniform was a perfect fit for him. His hair was freshly cut. He smiled when he saw me. I stood up and reached my hand out for him to shake. "How're you doing, David?"

David replied, "I'm good, Zin — Ms. Carter." And took his seat. "How are you?"

With a smirk on my face, I told David, "Listen, I know that you found a way to talk to Quran, so, you know good and well how I'm doing."

"True dat, but I had to ask, right? I was supposed to ask."

"I guess — but on a serious note, the U.S. Attorney's office has been silent in regards to you. I haven't heard anything from them about anything. And that worries me. Greg Gamble has a hard on for you, Quran, Jihad, my father and even me. But so far, I haven't heard shit from them."

"I heard through the grapevine that your father is over at the jail and has a hearing come up that might free him."

"He has a hearing coming up but him being freed is up to the judge. And if Greg Gamble has any say in it, that won't happen. Speaking of Gamble, Nikki Locks came to see me a couple days ago and she mentioned something about somebody in Gamble's office wanting to reopen your old murder case. Have you heard anything about that?"

"Who would I hear it from?" Dave asked defensively. "The only people I talk to are street niggas and you. I get all of my info from you."

"I know, but — damn. I don't even know if they can do that. And from what Nikki says, it's not even about you. It's about them wanting Quran for killing all of your witnesses. They also think he killed that woman named Tosheka."

"Why would anybody think that? Que loved Tosheka..."

The expression on my face changed.

51

"Once. He loved her once, before you came along. Why would he kill her?"

"I asked him and he denied doing it. I believe him."

"As you should. Que ain't gon lie. If he did something, he'd admit it."

"I believe that, too. But I'm still concerned about the bullseye that on his back. Greg Gamble framed my father back in the day. He might do the same thing to Quran. Well, anyway, I've been making my rounds, seeing all my clients and you're the last one here. Anthony Williams sends his love and respects. Said to tell you to 'Live The Omerta' and 'Death before Dishonor.' Oh — and, Nikki is Javon Jarrett's lawyer. She asked me if you were going to press charges against Jarrett."

"Tell that white bitch to suck my..."

"Hey, hey," I said and put my palms up. "Play nice."

"Ain't nobody playing with her ass. Fuck she gonna ask some stupid ass shit like that for? What did you tell her?"

"To suck your joint."

David laughed at my attempt at humor.

"Naw, for real though, I just told her that you didn't want to press charges and that you had no statements. That you don't know Jarrett or if he was actually the person who assaulted you."

"Good. I'ma see him again one day. And when I do..."

"Hey." I said, cutting David off. "I wish you wouldn't have assaulted Warren Stevenson. Who cares if he..."

"I cared, Zin!" David exclaimed. "I cared! He was disrespecting me as a man. No cold-blooded man should have to look at another man play with his dick in public just because they in jail. Pervert ass niggas can't control their sexual urges. He was jackin' off on the CO bitches in the bubble, but was hitting my head at the same time. I blanked. Got on his creep ass. So be it! I'ma live with the repercussions."

"Aight, tough guy, see if it'll be hard living with the fact that your ass could've been home right now, but now you're fighting another case. Especially if what the rumors been saying is true in regards to the U.S. Attorney's office trying to reopen the Solomon Robinson case. They might have a new witness..."

"Ain't no new witnesses. We don't leave witnesses."

"Okay. I hear you. Is there anything that you need from me before I leave?"

David stood up to leave. "Naw, I'm good. Just tell Que to be safe out there and we heard about the Sean Branch storm that's brewing. Tell him that I said to find shelter in the storm. Take care, Ms. Carter."

***

Inside my car, still parked in the parking lot in front of CTF, I was riveted to my seat, deep in thought. The night Quran killed his brother Khitab came to mind. Something that his brother had said...

"There's a lot of shit that you don't know, Que. Dave is jealous of you, and he's gonna cross you..."

"He's gonna cross me and you were the only one who could see it. So, to protect me, you ratted on him to the cops? Is that what you're tryna say, Tab?"

"Yes — no. Que, there's a lot more to it. You have to let me down and hear me out."

"Let you down, huh? Dave was gonna cross me? Did the cops tell you that?"

"I knew it before I came across the cops. I tried..."

"You know that Dave was gonna cross me and you kept that a secret!"

"I told you, bruh, there's a lot that you don't know."

"And how exactly was he gonna cross me, Tab? How was Dave gonna cross me?"

Khitab Bashir had never revealed to Quran what he knew. Even after Quran had asked him several times to tell him how David had planned to cross him. Khitab had known something that he wasn't saying. And Quran had impatiently killed his brother to right a perceived wrong that to Quran was worse than death. I sat back in the car seat and wondered what Khitab Bashir had known and wouldn't say. I thought about David Battle, my client and all the times I'd visited with him. I thought about Quran Bashir, the man I loved, the father of my unborn child and hoped that he knew what he was doing. I prayed that Khitab had been lying about David. I prayed that if anybody crossed anybody, Quran would survive when all the dust settled. Quran had to survive. He had to.

Chapter 8

Sean Branch
44th and Hayes St. NE

"Slim, you should've been fuckin' with me." Jacob 'Jakey' Gibson said. "I told you that Bosco gun supply couldn't fuck with mine. I got a white boy stationed out in Andrews that loves to fuck young black bitches. Up in the Heights, we got plenty of them around." Jakey laughed. "I get him plenty of pussy and he supplies me with guns and ammo. I got all top of the line shit. C'mon."

Jakey led me into the only building on Hayes Street. It was surrounded on both sides by private homes and looked like a suburban neighborhood. On the second floor, we stopped at an apartment at the end of the hall. Jakey pulled out the keys and opened the apartment door. Inside the apartment were several people. I did a quick mental count. Three men in the living room playing video games. Two women at the dining room table drinking and rolling jays of weed. Five people in the living room. I was led down a hallway to a bedroom. I noticed another bedroom door across from the one I entered. That door was closed. I wondered if there was someone in it. Inside the bedroom where Jakey led me to, it was sparsely furnished. Only a bed and nightstand next to the bed was all that was there. A big screen TV was mounted to the wall. Jakey went to the room's closet and dragged out two large duffle bags. He unzipped them both to reveal his wares.

"All this shit is military grade, Teflon. Ain't nobody in the city got this shit," Jakey boasted.

Jakey had done time with me in the Feds and knew my whole story. He'd been my celly in Lewisburg in 2003 before the riot with the Mexicans. He was one of the only people I knew who called me Teflon.

"I got rifles. Real sniper joints, too. Blackwater firearms, Brownings, Cadex Defense CDX's, Desert Techs, Franklin's, Israeli joints, Patriots, Springfield Armory's and Weatherby Mark 5's. I got shotguns, slim. Charles Daly's, Euro American Armory's, Franchi Affinity, Mossberg's, Tristar Arms, and Winchesters. I got choppers and every kind of handgun you can think of with all the sexy attachments, too. I got bullets to fit everything in here. They free with your purchase."

"Damn, Ock, you doing it big. Never knew you was holding like this."

"Go 'head with that bullshit, Teflon. When you first got home, I reached out to you and told you to pull up. The next thing I know, I hear that you was fuckin' with the competition. I was feeling some kind of way for a minute, but then I remembered that we brothers and that money don't change love that's been nurtured and built over time and hardship. Bosco getting whacked sent you back in my direction and I'm glad to have you here. Glad to see you and glad that we can do business." Jakey leaned down and rifled through one of the bags. "I got something here that I want you to see. It's..."

I shot Jakey in the back of the head twice and watched his body fall on the bags of guns. The sound suppressor on the barrel of the gun was a complement of Bosco. I pulled the second suppressed gun out of my pocket and waited to see if anyone came near the room. No one did. With all the racket going on in the living room, no one had heard a thing. I smiled to myself and left the room. First, I checked the bathroom. Empty. I wanted to check that bedroom, but neutralizing the threats in the living room had to come first. At the end of the hallway, I peeked around the corner. Everyone was where they'd been minutes ago. Two dudes on a couch. One in a chair next to the couch. I appeared in the open like a ghost and shot all three dudes. One of the women screamed. I silenced her next. Her body flew out of the chair at the table and hit the wall.

"Please... Please... don't kill me!" The other woman pleaded. "I didn't see anything. I swear, I didn't. I won't talk. Nobody will..."

I shot the woman in the face. Turning on my heels, I went to the bedroom with the closed door. I put one of the guns away, then covered my hand with my coat sleeve. The doorknob wouldn't turn. It was locked. I shot the lock and the doorknob off the door, then I kicked the door open. The room was empty. Furnished, but empty. I quickly searched the room. Under the bed were more duffle bags. Inside the closet were two more. Smiling to myself, I couldn't believe my good fortune. The two duffle bags under the bed were filled with money and the bags in the closet were filled with bullets, beams, extended clips, laser sightings for rifles, tripods, scopes, suppressors. I rummaged through the bag and stopped suddenly. I couldn't believe my eyes.

I reached down and grabbed a baseball sized object from the bag. Turning it over in my hand, it was the first real one I'd ever seen. "Jakey, you wild muthafucka," I mouthed to myself and saw at least five more objects in the bag like the one in my hand. I couldn't help but laugh. At a time like this when I was beefing with life itself, the universe had chosen to give me hand grenades. All I could do was laugh.

***

Early the next morning...
Alexandria, Virginia

"You cut your beard," Liv said as soon as I walked into her house. When I didn't respond, she said, "I been calling your phone since you left that night. I been worried sick about you."

"I couldn't protect my daughter, Liv. Somebody killed Shontay because of something I did. Do you understand how hard that is to live with?"

"Sean, please, baby, I..."

"You what, Liv? You've lost a child to violence? You watched your mother agonize over her grandchild, blame you for her death and then kill herself in front of you? Has that ever happened to you?"

Bolivia never responded.

"That's what I thought. I love you, Liv, but I can't protect you..."

"I don't need you to protect me!" Liv shouted.

"Yes, you do. Everybody around me is a target, Liv. Even you. You're not exempt because nobody hardly knows about you. About us. Niggas don't give two fucks about killing you to get to me. And I can't let that happen. I love you too much to let that happen. I couldn't protect Shontay, but I can protect you by leaving you alone. I have to get as far away from you as I can. And you have to accept that. Understand that. You have a long life to live, and you'll only shorten your lifespan if I stay with you. My heart is broken, Liv. What's left of it, anyway. I can't be the man that you need me to be when I'm so broken. So filled with pain, anger and vengeance. I killed six innocent people last night, Liv. I know that they were innocent, but I didn't care. I needed something that one of them had. I couldn't leave him around to tell the story.

"I killed him first. The other five people all died because they were there. Wrong place, wrong time. I got everything that I went there to get, Liv, and took six lives in the process. And guess what? I don't fuckin' feel a thing. I feel no remorse. No guilt. Nothing. Watching my mother put that gun in her mouth and pull the trigger changed me. Made me more animalistic. I'm completely devoid of emotion now. I cried my eyes out earlier today and I vowed to myself that I'd never shed another tear. But others will. The depth of my desire for destruction knows no limits, has no bounds. I came here to tell you all of this in person. Not over the phone. Felt like I owed you that much. I want you to keep the Porsche, Liv. It's paid for. It's yours. Keep all of my clothes and things, too. I might come back and need them one day. If I ever make it back here, it'll be to stay with no worries, no regrets, no vengeance."

Liv stood in the middle of the floor and cried her eyes out. "Sean, I love you. I love you. I love you."

Ignoring Liv's last words, I moved past her and gathered the things that I'd need to keep. When I got back to the living room, Liv was laying on her couch with her face covered by her arms. I could hear her pain, but I couldn't feel it. I felt nothing. Made myself feel nothing. I was an animal. I was a machine. I left Liv's house without another word. At the Porsche, I transferred all the bags to the van parked in Liv's garage. A van that I knew one day would come in handy. I tossed the bags from Liv's house in beside the ones I'd taken from Jakey's spot. I glanced back once at Liv's town house. I spotted Liv's face in the window. Her eyes full of tears as she watched me leave.

***

"Here's the key to your new storage unit, sir," the receptionist at EZ storage said.

"Thank you," I replied and walked away.

After loading all of the bags of weapons and money inside the storage room, I laid down beside the bags and went to sleep.

***

Sunny's Carry Out
5200 Blk of Sherriff Road
Northeast, DC

The turkey bacon, egg and cheese croissant was delicious. I sipped the lemonade and iced tea mix from the Styrofoam cup. I scanned the area in all directions but saw no obvious danger or threats. In that parking lot, I allowed myself the opportunity to strategize.

In my head, I tallied the list of my enemies. The list was a long one. I thought about all the people I'd killed since getting out of prison. That list was even longer. I did a mental count. Twenty-six. I had killed twenty-six people since my release from prison. As I chewed the second croissant, I said their names to myself. "Reese. Raquel. Tracy Kay. Frank Bailey. Eric Kay. Rick Bailey. Leon Clea. Stephen Hartwell. Moe Brooks. Frank Johnson. Kenny Sparrow. Byron 'Crud' Clark. Pig. Eric Ford. Blast. Silk. Derrick Hill. Tony Fortune. Trina Boo. Moe Best. Jakey. The five people in the apartment with Jakey." Then I did a process of elimination exercise in my head.

Raquel or Reese didn't have anyone to avenge them. The Kay niggas Eric and Tracy had another brother, James, but he was gay and no one knew I had killed Eric and Tracy. There was only speculation. Leon Clea had a brother named Andre Clea who'd been home from prison for about three years. He was a known killer who'd definitely want revenge about his brother. I filed the name Andre Clea into a different category. The category that meant death was coming soon. The cousins Frank and Rick Bailey had mostly women in their family. Stephen Hartwell, Frank Johnson and Moe Brooks were buried in shallow graves in the woods at Fort Dupont Park. No one knew where they were and who had killed them. Crud's two sisters went on the same list as Andre Clea. Pig didn't have a relative I could remember. Neither did Eric Ford. Leonard 'Silk' Johnson and Derrick Hill's deaths were open cases. Nobody knew I'd killed them.

Then I remembered something. Rodney Shaw knew. Rodney knew that me and Quran killed Baby E, Silk and Derrick. And Rodney knew I had a daughter. I put Rodney's name in the 'Die Soon' category and made a mental note to check and see if I needed to hunt Derrick Hill, Silk and Baby E's relatives. Tony Fortune had no sons or brothers left. Only the surviving daughter. I put her on the list with the others. I had let her live the night the others died in the Copper Canyon Grill parking lot. That had been a mistake. One that I promised myself to rectify.

Trina Boo's son, Lil' Mike went on the list, but I didn't put Trina's daughter Tiera on it. Didn't feel the need to just yet. The last person's name on the list of people I'd killed *before* Shontay's death was Moe Best. And Moe Best had brothers who'd definitely want to avenge him. Namely Kenny and Jew Bay. I put both Best brothers on the list of those who'd die soon. Although, no one could say for sure that I killed Moe Best... then a thought hit me. Somebody did know that I *wanted* to kill Moe Best. My lil' homie Rebo. Rico and Raphael's younger brother. Had Rebo talked about the day I had stalked Moe Best and had given him that ARP? I never told him what I wanted with Moe Best and just to call me if he saw him.

Rico Thomas and Raphael Parker were my men, but if I start to think that it was Rebo who told people in the neighborhood that I was looking for Moe and he'd probably killed him, then Rebo's name would have to go on that list. The Best family knew I had a daughter named Shontay and they probably knew she worked at Chipotle. "Fuck it, I'ma put their whole family on the list."

The next names that came to mind made me smile. Bionca Clark. Brechelle Clark. Renaissance Tyler. I added the three women to my list of people who'd die as soon as possible. Finishing off the iced tea, lemonade mix I put all of the trash back in the bag and tossed it out the window. The first stop on my list was Clay Terrace. Crossing my fingers, I prayed that Rodney Shaw was outside in the area somewhere. I needed to kill him first. If I can't find Rodney, my next destination will be Southern Avenue. The two Clark sisters, Bionca and Brechelle, needed to join their brothers and mother.

Chapter 9
Bionca Clark

Celine James swept into the restaurant like a whirlwind. Her blonde weave was on point and she tossed it to and fro like she knew she was a bad bitch. Celine's jeans hugged her every curve. Her beige Ugg boots matched the beige cashmere trench-like coat that she wore. Hers was a face that didn't need make up, but light pink gloss adorned Celine's lips anyway. She spotted me at the table and headed my way. I stood to embrace Celine, then took my seat at the table again.

"I guess you just decided to return my calls and texts," Celine said as soon as she was seated.

"Don't start that shit, Celine. You already know my life been hectic as shit for about the last month. I haven't been communicating with anyone."

Celine removed her coat and sat her purse on the table. "I do know and that's why I'm here and didn't ignore your texts and calls. Plus you know how I feel about these cheeseburgers at Capital Burger. Did you order yet? I'm hungry as shit."

"Naw. I was waiting for you to get here before I ordered," I replied and signaled the female waitress nearby.

"Good afternoon, ladies. What can I get you today?" The waitress asked.

Celine smiled and said, "I'll have the double cheeseburger with the aged balsamic mushrooms, fried egg and smoked bacon. French fries crispy and an apple Sexy Nipple."

"Damn, bitch, you drinkin' early, ain't you?" I said to Celine. To the waitress, I said, "I'll have the steakhouse cheeseburger and the loaded fries. And I'll take the same drink she's having, the Sexy Nipple, but make mine a watermelon one."

"I'll be back soon with your drinks, ladies."

As soon as the waitress was out of earshot, Celine said, "Let those without sin cast the first stone."

"This sinner right here says if you can't beat them, join them."

Celine laughed. "Bionca, I'm really sorry about Brion and Ms. Barbara."

"Yeah, me too, but you left somebody out, didn't you?"

"I'd never wish death on nobody, but you already know that I hated Crud."

"A lot of people did, I hear. It's cool, though."

"And that's fucked up what happened to Tosheka."

"Tell me about it."

"How is Bree holding up?"

"She's as good as can be. She stayed in Carolina after she buried my mother there. She ain't coming back here. Too many bad memories."

"I don't blame her." Celine said.

"Me, either." I replied.

The waitress returned and sat a drink in front of the both of us. Then she disappeared as quickly as she'd come.

I sipped my drink. "Damn, that's good."

Celine sipped hers, licked her pouty lips and said, "I know, right?"

"I missed you, Celine."

"You got me feeling like a ping pong ball, Bionca. You killing me with this wishy-washy shit. Sometimes you want me, sometimes you don't. I'm not a fuckin' slinky. Or better yet, a human Etch and Sketch where you draw my heart on the screen and then shake it up and erase it minutes later. You throwing me the fuck off. I swear to God."

"I still miss you."

"Fuck you, Bionca. Fuck you."

"You miss me?"

"No."

"*Liar*!"

***

"Don't lick my pussy real slow like that, Bionca! Shit feels too good! You gon' drive me crazy!"

I ignored Celine as I lay between her outstretched legs. I focused on the bottom of her wet pussy and tongue-kissed her there. Slowly, I made my way up.

"I wanna taste you, too! Let me taste you!" Celine begged. "I wanna suck on you, Bionca! Let me do it!"

Say less, I thought then positioned myself in 69. I lowered my wetness onto Celine's mouth and let her do her. Celine clutched my legs to hold me in place as she ate me like a famished refugee. In minutes, I was coming all over her face. I thought that Celine wouldn't let up and be satisfied with just me pleasing her, but that wasn't the case. Before long, our roles reversed and I was the one begging for Celine to stop sucking on my clit. But my pleas fell on deaf ears. I cried out and wiggled and squirmed to escape her skillful tongue, but Celine wasn't having none of it. So, I gave up and gave in to the intense pleasure I was enveloped in. I squeezed my eyes shut and had multiple orgasms with Celine. But the entire time I was in Celines' bed, I wished that she was Ren.

***

"If the house on Southern Avenue feels like it got ghosts in it, where the hell you been staying at?" Celine asked while drying off. She'd just gotten out of the shower.

"Brion's girlfriend Ren has been taking his death super hard. Harder than me. And I think she's suicidal. Well, I know she is. I had to pull her ass out of her bathtub before she drowned in it. She took something and tried to say she didn't. Plus, she's pregnant..."

"By Brion?"

I nodded. "Never even got the chance to tell him about it. I been over her house. Haven't been home since my mother passed. I need to go by there and grab some things. Can you go with me?"

"Of course, I can. When?"

"As soon as I get dressed."

***

"Overcast skies." Celine observed as we exited her building. "Looks like it's been raining."

"Let's take your car. I like the tints." I said.

"Cool."

We hopped into Celine's 5 Series Benz and hit the road. I leaned back in the passenger seat and let the music that came through the car's speakers relax me more than the multiple orgasms I'd had. Mary J. Blige's voice was melodic, angelic...

"I'm not in love/it's just some kinda thing I'm going through/going through, going through/and it's not infatuation/ain't nothing going on between me and you/me and you, me and you/but I dream about it every night/wanting you here with me/making love tome/and oh/I'm missing you like crazy/my soul is aching/I'm out of control/missing you so/I'm missing you/missing you/I'm missing you/I'm not in love/that's what I keep telling myself/over and over again/and I'm not the least bit amused

by it, baby/yet I don't want to be with nobody else/no, no, no/and I dream about you all the time/touching and kissing me/and making love to me..."

The lyrics to the Mary J. Blige songs seemed to apply to my life, but I was confused about who I wanted it to apply to. Celine or Ren. Was it possible for me to be in love with Ren? "Put some GoGo in," I told Celine to rid myself of my thoughts. As the music changed to *Familiar Faces*, I snapped out of my funk and thought about what Ren and I had accomplished. We'd found Sean Branch's daughter and killed her. And we were rewarded with a two for one situation. After learning about her granddaughter's murder, Sean's mother, Sharon Branch had taken her own life. We'd seen the story on the news. Ren and I had celebrated by drinking Patron and smoking. Now, all we had to do was find Sean and kill him. I opened my eyes in time to see my house appear in view. "Pull in behind that burgundy caravan." Celine did as instructed. Seeing the family home brought on too many memories at once. I sat in my seat and stared at it.

"Are you okay, Bionca?" Celine asked.

"Naw, not really." I replied

"Can't do it, huh?"

I shook my head. "I guess not. I'm not ready to go in there just yet. I can't."

"Want me to go in and get what you need? You know I know the whole layout of the house and I've been in your room a thousand times. Just tell me what you need and where it's at and I'll get it. Okay?"

"Okay," I replied and told Celine everything I wanted her to grab for me. "There's a Louis Vuitton duffle in the closet. Get that and put everything in there."

"Aight. I got you," Celine said and reached for the door handle.

"How are you gon' get in without the keys, goofy ass?" I joked and fished my house keys out of my pocket. "Here.

And it's starting to rain again. Put my hat on." I took off my Channel pulldown hat and passed it to Celine.

"Thanks, bitch. Can't fuck up this thousand-dollar Indian weave." Celine pinned her hair up and put the Channel hat on over it.

I watched Celine cross the street to the house and then closed my eyes.

The unmistakable sounds of gunshots rang out. I opened my eyes and saw a black clad figure standing over Celines fallen body. She had made it to my front door. As I watched in horror, sparks erupted from the gun's barrel as bullets slammed into Celine. I wanted to scream, but I couldn't. All I could do was watch.

Chapter 10
Ren Tyler

Completely nude, I stood in front of the full-length mirror and eyed my body. The tattoos, the piercings, the curly bush growing above my pussy. That drew my attention to the tattoo of Brion's name on my pelvis area. The hair growing in that area was covering parts of the tattoo. Quickly, I went to the bathroom and got my razor, shaving cream, and a wet washcloth. I shaved the curly bush from the region in minutes. Once completely bald, I rubbed the platinum bar piercing that went through my clit. It matched the ones in my nipples and navel.

"You need the whole set, baby."

I could hear Brion's voice in my head. A life taken, a life given. I wiped the excess cream from my body with the hot, wet washcloth, then put it and the razor on the dresser. On the dresser was the pregnancy test applicator with positive results. I'd kept it to show it to Blast but never got the chance to. I picked up the applicator and looked at it. The bright pink plus sign was still visible. My tears started then and I didn't bother to wipe them away. I thought about the fetus that I had aborted at thirteen. The product of a violent rape. This pregnancy was the exact opposite of that one. This one was born out of love. Deep love. Although tragedy would mar the arrival of the child, it was what I needed. Something besides tattoos and piercing and pictures to remind of Brion.

I eyed the colorful assorted flowers that started at my right shoulder and extended down my rib cage and stomach. I eyed the rest in peace tattoo across my breast that had Von Tyler's sunrise and sunset dates. The tattoos on my rib cage merged with the flames on my back. I had to get a handheld mirror to use with the full-length mirror in order to see the portrait of Brion now tattooed on my back. The likeness on my back was breathtaking.

Before I knew it, my hormones raged. I put down the handheld mirror and closed my eyes. I imagined Brion with his hands on me, his tongue. I squeezed my hand between my legs as my fingers explored my center. The wetness surprised me as it gushed out onto my finger. I thought about Brion's tongue on my toes as he licked and kissed my feet.

I saw him kiss the ever-present anklet on my ankle before he'd enter me. Slipping two fingers inside me, I wanted to feel his thickness. I added a third finger to stretch my wall like Brion often did.

"Oooowww," I moaned as I tried to put all three fingers as far as they could go inside me. "Blast... baby!"

BOOM! BOOM! BOOM! BOOM!

Startled, my neck almost snapped as it whipped around to the sounds of the banging on my apartment door.

"The fuck...?" I uttered as I pulled my fingers from inside me and wiped them with the washcloth on the dresser. Quickly, I grabbed my robe and put it on, tying it as I crossed the room and got one of my guns out. I thought for a moment of the police, but shook that thought from my head as I walked through the living room towards the door. I looked out the peephole and saw Bionca's face. Stepping back, I swung the door open. "Fuck you banging on the door like that for?"

Bionca moved past me in a blur. She shed her coat and turned to face me. Her eyes were full of tears.

"Bionca... What's wrong? What happened?"

"He killed her."

70

"He killed who? And who's he that killed someone?"

"Celine. Sean Branch killed Celine," Bionca said and fell on the couch. She covered her eyes and cried.

"Who is Celine, Bionca? And how do you know that Sean Branch killed her?" I asked in rapid succession.

Bionca used both hands to wipe her eyes. She looked at me, but her eyes were void, sullen. "Celine is Celine James. My on-again, off-again girlfriend..."

"Girlfriend? I didn't know..."

"There's a lot about me that you don't know, Ren. I needed someone to relieve my stress, so I called Celine. It's been months since I last saw her or spoke to her. Went to Capital Burger on Seventh Street for lunch. I told Celine to meet me there. She did. We went to Celine's after eating. We chilled for a minute. Then I told Celine to take me to the house; to *my* house. Told her I needed to pick up some stuff. We rode there in Celine's BMW. At the house, I got... I got goosebumps and was scared to go inside. So, I sent Celine into the house. It was raining a little bit, so I gave Celine my hat to wear over her weave. I closed my eyes for a second. A quick second. When I opened them, I saw the man in all black shoot Celine... over and over and over again." Bionca broke down then.

I stood in my spot and kept quiet. Let her get her tears out. I figured that Bionca would speak again when she was ready. It was the same thing I did when Brion was hurting about something.

"I watched that man stand over Celine and kill her! He thought she was me! He thought it was me! Sean was at the house waiting for me. As soon as Celine walked up to the front door, he was on her. It was supposed to be me!"

"How do you know it was Sean Branch, though, Bionca? Was he bare-faced when he did it?"

"No. He wasn't. And I didn't see his face from my seat in the car. But I know it was him. I'm sure of it. It was him."

"But, if you didn't see..."

"*Ren, it was fuckin' him, okay? It was him!*"

"Okay, okay. If you say so."

"I say so, god dammit! It was him. Who else could it be? Who else would want to kill me? Be at my house waiting on me? Who?"

"But, how would he know..."

"Know what, Ren? Where I lived? Who I was?"

"Yeah... I mean, how would he know about you that fast and post up outside your house to kill you? And for what? Why would he want to kill you so bad? Do you think he knows that you and I killed his daughter? If so, then that means he knows about me, too, then, right?

Before Bionca could answer me, my cellphone rang. I walked over and picked it up. Answered it. "Hello... what? How? No... no... no..." I threw the cellphone across the room. "No-no- no— It can't be! Can't be!"

Bionca was up off the couch in seconds and standing in front of me. "Ren, what...? What was that call about?"

"My mother's house just blew up. As my cousin Dame ran out of the house, someone shot him. He's dead."

"Was your mother home?"

"No. She was at work. Dame was there alone."

"I'm sorry to hear about your cousin, Ren, but does that answer any of your questions?"

"You think it was Sean Branch who did that? Went to my mother's house and killed Dame?

"Unless your mother or cousin got enemies like ours, it was him. He went there looking for you, hours after he left my house thinking he killed me."

"But... but... how could he know..."

"Where your mother lives? Know about you killing his daughter?"

I nodded my head. "How could he know?"

Chapter 11

Det. Bob Mathis
Violent Crimes Branch
Pennsylvania Ave. SE
Hours later...

"Who ordered the pizza?" Detective Rio Jefferson asked the room.

"The pizza would be me," Detective Corey Winslow responded.

"The Chinese takeout?"

I stepped up and grabbed the Wa Sin carryout bag from Rio. I looked in the bag to make sure that everything I ordered was there.

"Uh... pasta and wings from Pizza Boli's?"

Detective Matt Arnold appeared out of nowhere. "I'm right here, buddy. Let me get that baked Ziti and garlic pepper wings. Is there a soda in the bag?"

Rio Jefferson looked in the bag. "Yes, there is, kind sir." He handed the bag to Matt. "Greek cuisine from some place I can't even pronounce."

"Give me my shit, Jefferson," Phil Krause said.

"Temper, temper, big guy. We know you get moody when you're hungry."

"The America's Best Wings bag is mine, so this must be yours, Hackett," Rio said and passed the Panera Bread bag to Detective Nate Hackett. "Bag feels kinda light, Hack."

"Trying to watch my figure, Rio," Nate Hackett replied.

Everybody dug into their food and quiet filled the room.

***

"Okay," I said after cleaning my hands. "What do we have on the board?"

"Everything," Rio Jefferson answered.

"We got some new shit that I think you'll be interested in, Bob."

"Give it to me," I replied.

"Aight, here it goes. Officers responded to a shooting in the 5000 block of D Street in southeast yesterday and found a man suffering from gunshot wounds. He died at the scene. Smiley radios me and sends me to the scene. The man has identification in his pocket. Turns out to be 30-year-old Michael Jones. Name sound familiar to you, Bob?"

"Michael Jones?" I repeated. "Thirty years old. Naw, should it?"

"If his name doesn't ring a bell, his mother's name sure will. Trina Boo."

I came forward in my chair rapidly. "Michael Jones is Trina Boo's son?"

"The one and only," Corey Winslow chimed in. "How suspicious is that? Woman gets killed with a known rat in a rinky-dink hotel in Maryland and then a week later, her son is killed on his block. No motive."

"Any witnesses?"

"Several. They say that Mike was gambling with friends moments before a lone gunman dressed in all black came out of nowhere and shot him. It wasn't random. Witnesses say that Michael Jones was definitely the target."

"Maybe he did something to somebody out of grief for his mother. Both murders don't have to be related," Nate Hackett said. "Shit like this happened before."

"Good point," I said. "Was anything found on his person?"

"ID, a debit card, wad of money... about three hundred or so dollars, a baggie of exotic weed, a cell phone... that's about it," Rio Jefferson said

"Well," Corey Winslow said, "I think the two murders are related. Just like the one earlier on Southern Avenue."

"Southern Avenue? What happened on Southern Avenue?" Phil Krouse asked.

"A young woman was killed on the front porch of 832 Southern Avenue."

"Brion and Byron Clark's mother's house," I said.

Corey Winslow nodded and so did Nate Hackett.

"The woman hasn't been identified yet, but we believe it's Byron and Brion's sister Bionca."

"Someone's declared war on the whole fuckin' family!" Nate Hackett exclaimed. "I pulled video from several businesses near the parking lot in the rear of Stewart's funeral home and came up with nothing."

"Same here on Byron and Artinis Winston's murders on Third Street," Matt Arnold added. "Still haven't recovered Byron Clark's head, either."

"When will we have an ID on the woman killed on Southern Avenue?" asked Corey Winslow.

"Soon. And I saw cameras attached to homes on both sides of 832, so, hopefully, we'll get something useful from them. For those who don't know, this family has experienced tragedy after tragedy. Woman has four children, Byron Clark being the oldest. He's killed in the house on Third Street and beheaded. At the memorial... Byron was cremated... the younger brother, Brion Clark is shot and killed as he left the service. Then the mother, Barbara Clark has a heart attack on the spot and later dies at an area hospital the same night. The youngest daughter takes her mother's body to North Carolina to be buried and stays there. That leaves... one surviving child. Bionca Clark. And I think that's her over at the morgue. Shot and killed by a lone gunman dressed in black."

"Hey, that... you keep saying 'Lone gunman dressed in black'... makes me think about something a witness just told me at the Hayes Street massacre scene. Six people were shot to death in an apartment there. Nobody heard any gunshots at all or witnessed the murders. But an old lady who left the building that night remembers seeing a lone black man tossing duffle bags into a car. A sports car that was pretty nice. The old woman's words verbatim. Oh, and he was dressed in all black."

"No video at that scene?" I asked.

"Cameras attached to the building weren't working. Joe Haden and Ted Jonas are working the case full time. Just remembered the lone black man dressed in black part. Thought it might mean something," Rio Jefferson went on to say.

"This shit is getting repetitive and out of control. Look at all the open cases we got on the murder board." I pointed out.

"Hey," Corey Winslow said, "give me some fuckin' credit here, Bob, I'm the one who helped turn Luther 'Khadafi' Fuller. He's been spilling his guts to me and Ann Sloan for months now. In May, he'll testify against Antonio Felder and that alone will close almost forty murders..."

"Cold case murders," Rio Jefferson stated. "Not new ones. Like the ones up there on the murder board. We gotta solve recent murders and put criminals away for committing those murders. Unless, Corey here wants to bargain with all murder suspects and let them back on the street because they turn rat."

"You got something you want to say to me, Rio?" Corey Winslow bellowed. "Something you wanna get off your chest?"

"I just did. Besides, everybody in this room already know how I feel about the fuckin' deal you made with Khadafi Fuller. Despite the fact that he's responsible for one of our colleagues' deaths. Maurice Tolliver deserved better..."

"Hey!" I exploded. "Put a fuckin' sock in it, you two! This ain't the time nor place to rehash all that shit! We have a serial killer on the loose named Sean Branch and we need to focus on finding him and stopping him. Any new leads in his daughter's murder?"

Nobody spoke up and said anything.

"Anything new about Quran Bashir?" I asked.

Again nothing was said.

"Phil, gaining any ground in the Denico Autrey and Bole Ndugo case?"

"Nothing new, Bob," Phil Krouse replied.

"Fuck!" I muttered and looked again at the murder board. I stared at the names of all the dead. Lost souls who depended on the men in that room to find their killers. I looked at the faces of each detective present. Then I shook my head. "Un-fuckin'-believable!"

Chapter 12

Michael Carter
Three Days Later...
DC Superior Court
501 Indiana Avenue
9:03 A.M.

"...Hope Village gotta let you out in your first seven days for a religious service. Whatever your religion is, they gon' let you go out. So, I put in to go to Jumah the first Friday I got there. I was tryna go to the Masjid out of Glenarden, but they want you go to 18th and Monroe. Cool. I agreed to that, got my paper and bounced. The 18th and Monroe Masjid is small, but it be packed like hell. All throwback Lorton niggas and niggas that been in the Feds. I call it the convict Masjid. Anyway, slim, I'm in the joint, glad to be at Jumah in the free world after doing fourteen years in jail. I'm sitting upstairs on the top-level listening to the Khutbah. I don't even know none of the brothers' names in there, but the Khutbah was like that. After the Khutbah, we offer the prayer and then it's over. You know me, I'm tryna hurry up and get my pass signed by somebody... one of the brothers, so that I can bounce and go see my lil' young joint Randi on Howard Road. Slim... I get in the office where they signing the passes and you ain't gon' believe who signing the passes."

"Who, slim? Who signing 'em?"

"Pappy!"

"Pappy? Jermaine Vick? From 15th Place?"

"Fuck yeah!"

"Naw, slim! You bullshittin'!"

"Wallahi."

"That's crazy!" The dudes said and laughed.

"I know, right?"

"What did you do? I know you said something."

"Shid. Nigga, I ain't retarded or crazy. I'm hip to slim. I'm standing there in line tryna get my pass signed. Ain't but one halfway house in the city. He knew where the fuck I was. You think I'ma say something to that man, disrespect that man knowing that he's a killer and I'm a sitting duck in Hope Village? What did I do? Kept my muthafuckin' mouth closed and got my paper signed, then bounced. That's what the fuck I did. Fuck I'ma prove to the world by telling him he couldn't sign my paper because he's a rat and then he kill me? Niggas know what he did to Kevin and Asay 'nem and ain't nobody done nothing to him. Why should I jump out there? The man ain't hiding. He in the freakin' Masjid giving Khutbahs and signing halfway house papers. He's the assistant Imam in that joint. I did tell you that 18th and Monroe is filled every Friday with jail niggas, right? If the niggas that been with Kevin since Oak Hill and Ceder Knoll ain't tryna say nothing or do nothing to slim, why should I? Man, ain't nobody out there killing no rats no more..."

"I beg to differ, youngin'," I whispered to myself as I listened to the two dudes in the cage talk. I knew all the people the dude spoke about personally. Smiling to myself, I had to respect what the dude was saying. He would have marked himself for death had he said the wrong thing to Pappy. Pappy had dishonored himself by violating the code of silence, but his gun game was so wicked and his kill ratio was so high that nobody dared to do anything to him.

"Carter!" The Marshal appeared at the bars and called out.

I stood up and walked to the front of the holding cage.

"Come on, Carter. It's time for court."

"Good luck, old head," the dude who'd been talking moments ago said.

"Thanks, youngin'. I'ma need it," I replied and left the cage.

The Marshal was white and built like a linebacker in the NFL. His clothes hugged his body too snug. He reminded me of Howie Long. Buzz haircut and all. The Marshal led me through a labyrinth of hallways until we reached an elevator. "Your first time in front of Judge Hamilton, Carter?"

I nodded my head.

"You ever heard what they call him?"

I had heard what Judge Hamilton was called, but I played coy. "Naw, what?"

"Cut 'Em Loose Bruce. You lucked up when you drew Judge Hamilton to preside over your evidentiary hearing. Been in jail since 1995, huh, Carter?"

I nodded again.

The elevator door opened and we stepped on.

"A lot in the world has changed since then. Especially here in DC. The only thing that hasn't changed is the Redskins winning a Superbowl since 1992."

I laughed at that.

The elevator sounded and the door opened. The Marshal put me into a small cage. "Hopefully, things work out for you, Carter. I believe that every man deserves a second chance at redemption. Your lawyers will be back here shortly to talk to you. Good luck, big guy."

Lawyers. "Thanks, man. I appreciate that."

Five minutes later, Jon Zucker walked through the door that led to the courtroom. "Mike, how you doing, buddy?" Jon asked.

"I'm good, Jon. Ready to get to it," I replied

"So am I, so am I. You must have powerful friends somewhere that you never mentioned to me, Mike."

Confused, I asked Jon, "Why do you say that?"

"Because one of the most respected criminal defense attorneys in the nation contacted me two days ago and asked if he could sit in on your hearing as co-counsel. Before I could decline, I was faxed a motion from Judge Hamilton granting the addition of J. Alexander Williams..."

"Who?"

"J. Alexander Williams. In legal circles, he's called the new Johnny Cochran."

"And he's on my case?"

"Yep. Don't know who sent him or what he's supposed to do for you. All I know is that he's here and he's your lawyer, too. I talked to him and he's only saying that he was sent by a priest to advise me in the hearing. I didn't even know that you were Catholic."

"Shit. Neither did I," I said, knowing now that Carlos Trinidad had sent the top gun attorney to assist Jon Zucker. He wanted me to be freed from prison. I was starting to think that maybe that wasn't a good thing.

"Well, in any event, Maryann Settles and her husband are out in the gallery ready to testify. I'm ready to get this ball rolling. Are you?"

"I'm ready," I said with confidence I really didn't feel.

"Aight. The Judge will be in at 9:30 and he'll call you in then," Jon Zucker told me and turned and left.

***

"Your Honor, I call to the stand, Maryann Settles," Jon Zucker announced.

Maryann Settles glanced at me and smiled as she walked past me to the witness stand. Being about my age or a little older, she'd aged well and looked pretty good. Nothing like the junkie crackhead she used to be. I looked back at the man sitting in the first row of the gallery seat. He watched Maryann attentively. Had to be the husband, Christopher.

"Please state your full name for the court, ma'am."

81

"Maryann Gisselle Settles."

Maryann Settles was duly sworn in by the clerk, then took her seat on the witness stand. She was dressed in multi-colored hospital scrubs and crocs.

"Mrs. Settles," Jon Zucker started, "I see that you're wearing hospital scrubs. What is your occupation?"

"I'm an LPN — Licensed Practitioner Nurse at Kaiser Permanente."

"And how long have you been in the healthcare field?"

"Ever since I got sober. So, it's been about eleven years now, I believe."

"Since you got sober you say? Can I ask what substances you abused?"

"You may ask. I was addicted to crack cocaine, prescription pills and heroin for most of my teenage years and adult life. There was a long road to recovery, but I'm blessed to have persevered."

"We are all glad you persevered, Mrs. Settles. Let me direct your attention to January 17th of 1996. Do you remember the events of that day?"

"I do."

"What do you remember about that day?"

"The jump out boys jumped out on me and caught me with a half a gram of heroin on Martin Luther King Jr. Avenue and Talbert Street. I was arrested and charged with possession with intent to distribute heroin. It was supposed to be charged as a simple possession..."

"Objection, Your Honor, speculative." Ian McNeely said.

"Sustained."

"Mrs. Settles, what was your mind state at the time of your arrest?"

"Fear. I was very afraid of going to prison... in the nineties back then, Lorton had a facility for women. I was afraid of going to Lorton's women prison."

"While incarcerated on those charges and scared of going to prison, did you have the opportunity to talk to someone?"

"Yes, I did."

"Was that person your lawyer?"

"No."

"Was that person a police officer?"

"No."

"Please tell this court who that person was that you ended up talking to."

"I talked to Gregory Gamble. A prosecutor at the United States Attorney's office."

"For the record, Mrs. Settles, would you tell the court where this meeting was."

"Your Honor, defense counsel is leading the witness. The witness never testified to a meeting taking place. Just that she talked to someone."

"Sustained." The Judge said. "Don't lead the witness, Mr. Zucker. Just ask your questions."

"Yes, sir, Your Honor. I'll rephrase the question. Mrs. Settles, you just testified to talking to AUSA Greg Gamble in 1996, correct?"

"That's correct."

"Do you remember where you were when you talked to him?"

"Yes. I was inside this building, in the rear of it somewhere. There's a holding section where all the women sit and wait to be called on by a lawyer. Before I could see or talk to a lawyer that day, I was taken to a small room somewhere. It was inside that small room that I talked to Greg Gamble."

Chapter 13
Zin
DC Superior Court
501 Indiana Avenue NW

By the time I walked into courtroom 511, the hearing was underway. There were so many prosecutors in the gallery seats that the courtroom could have been mistaken for the US Attorney's office conference room. I saw my father sitting at the defense table with Jon Zucker and a well-dressed black man who looked familiar, but I couldn't place his face. I removed my coat and found a seat at the rear of the courtroom. On the witness stand was Maryann Settles. Assistant United States Attorney Ian McNeely had the floor.

"Mrs. Settles, you testified that Greg Gamble, who as you say, was a regular prosecutor back then, that he told you that your charges would be dropped if you complied with his request, correct?"

"Correct."

"Were they dropped?"

"Yes."

"Your Honor, I'd like to enter exhibit 1-A into evidence," Ian McNeely said.

"Exhibit 1-A is entered. Proceed."

Ian McNeely walked up to Maryann Settles and presented her with a document.

"Mrs. Settles, can you please read what I just gave you?"

Maryann Settles read the document.

IF YOU CROSS ME ONCE 5 | ANTHONY FIELDS

"That document is an official document. It's headed 'DC Superior Court', right?"

"Right."

"Is that your name on the document and what you were charged with on January 17th, 1996?"

"I've never seen this paper before."

"I didn't ask you if you'd seen it before, I asked you is it accurate? Is that your name and what you were charged with on January 17th, 1996?"

"I think so... looks like it."

"On January 17th, 1996, you had more than one charge, correct?"

Maryann Settles was suddenly very rattled. Her face was a mask of confusion and annoyance. "I — uh — I – I don't remember..."

"You don't remember being charged with prostitution?"

"I - uh – it wasn't..."

"Mrs. Settles, please, take your time. Try and refresh your memory. You testified here today, and you also outlined in your affidavit that you were charged with drugs, but you omitted the fact that you were charged with prostitution."

"Objection, your honor!" Jon Zucker stood and said. "Relevance?"

"Your honor, this is about veracity. Truthfulness. Motive."

"Overruled. Continued, counselor."

"On January 17th you were observed to be involved in an illegal sex act in public. Officers saw you bent over a trash receptacle..."

"Your honor, this is unacceptable. The government is attempting to sully the witness..."

"Your honor," Ian McNeely interjected. "We are here to ascertain the truth. That's all. And the truth is in the files. Mrs. Settles has failed to mention — well, not even fail to mention, she's completely added her own version of what she was arrested for in January of 1996. The police reports..."

"You honor." Jon Zucker was livid. "The US attorney's office has failed to disclose any documents about Mrs. Settles' arrest on January 17th of 1996. We have not seen this document that the government has put forward as exhibit 1-A or any police reports related to Mrs. Settles arrest on January 17th, 1996..."

Judge Bruce Hamilton scoffed. "Let me see both counsel at the bench."

***

During a recess...

"Gamble and company blindsided us." Jon Zucker told me.

"It's a Brady violation," I replied.

"I know, but one that Bruce Hamilton is not going to rule on now. This thing gets reversed on appeal — if there is an appeal, but that only drags things out. We want to get Mike home now."

"This is a minor hiccup. It's not insurmountable," The well-dressed black man said.

I looked at him like he had antlers growing out of his head. "Excuse me, but you are? I never got your name."

"I'm sorry. Zinfandel Carter, right? My name is Jasper Alexander Williams. And I..."

"Wait, Jasper Alexander Williams? As in J. Alexander Williams?"

"Yes, ma'am. You've heard of me?"

I became starstruck like a young girl. My eyes widened. My tough facade folded. "Oh my gawd, you are a legend in black legal circles..."

"White legal circles, too," Jon Zucker said and smiled.

"I can't believe it. Why are you here? I mean, I'm glad that you're here. It's great to have met you in person, but really, why are you here sitting with Jon at my father's defense table?"

"Your father has very powerful allies, Ms. Carter. People I am not at liberty to mention or discuss, but I can say that they want to see your father go free. I was sent here by those people. And not to take anything away from Mr. Zucker — a highly skilled and competent attorney who I am very familiar with as well. I'm just here to add whatever legal advice I can give. This hearing has sort of a trial feel to it. How? Because the United States Attorney's Office felt it necessary to diminish Maryann Settles standing to the judge. They want to put Mrs. Settles on trial here so to speak. There are obvious and glaring violations by the USAO but there's no way to prove that Maryann Settles didn't see those charges on paper. This — these allegations if true — create a myriad of problems for the US Attorney's Office. They are going to defend themselves by using every dirty tactic that they have at their disposal. Here's what we do, on redirect, we acquiesce to the prostitution charge and chalk it up to past drug use, time and diminishing memory. What's clear is this, these allegations are there, and the burden of proof is on the government to prove that this didn't happen. They can't do that. Why? Because we'll hammer home the dates and times when vouchers were used to pay Mrs. Settles. We have a trail of receipts where money was paid."

"I think what the government attorney is doing is trying to paint Maryann Settles as a liar. Destroy her credibility in front of the judge. That's why they went right to it. First order of business. The reasoning is that if she's ashamed of the prostitution charge and or didn't tell her husband about it, she concealed it from him and us by not mentioning it in her affidavit. That gives her the proprietary to lie..."

"I agree with everything you just said, Ms. Carter and I hear that you are a great, young defense attorney in your own light. I appreciate and respect that. But, in my expert opinion, we don't need to overthink this. We simplify it and keep it that way. We focus on the affidavit and what's in it. Not what's not in it. That's what the government wants us to do. We stick to the facts. And those are that Maryann Settles is here in court today. Albeit, it's been seventeen years since she was last in one. She's here admitting to a crime. A crime that is punishable by five years in jail, which is the place that she lied to avoid eighteen years ago. She was not coerced or prodded by any investigators or the defendant to come forward. She did it on her own. We subpoena Gary Kohlman, if we have to, to tell the judge how he received the affidavit out the blue, certified mail. The fact that the mail went to his office all these years later instead of Mr. Zucker's proves that nobody on our side forced Mrs. Settles to come forward. Once we establish that, again, we stick to the facts. She was arrested and spoke to Greg Gamble. Her charges disappeared. She was allowed to go home and not jail. She testified falsely against Michael Carter. And she was paid to do so. Now, she wants to free the innocent man she lied on in 1996 at trial. Greg Gamble is scheduled to testify at this hearing."

"He's in the building," Jon Zucker said. "Saw him a few minutes ago, talking to Ian McNeely."

"Well," J. Alexander Williams continued, "He's a witness in this hearing. Mr. Zucker you get to officially tear him a new asshole."

"Oooh, I wish it was me. I swear to God."

***

"Mrs. Settles, you allege that you were paid this money..."

"I don't allege anything. I was paid."

"Yes, ma'am. If you say so. But I'm not disputing whether or not you were paid. What I want to clarify for this court, the reason for the payments. Do you have anything in writing — an agreement of any kind — that verifies the reason that you were paid this money?"

"No, I do not. He didn't give me any."

"So, it's your testimony, that you were paid this money by Greg Gamble — to lie and say that Michael Carter killed Dontay Samuels in 1995?"

"That's what I said. I've said it repeatedly."

"I understand that part, Mrs. Settles, but what I'm searching for is the truth."

"I'm telling the truth."

"So, you weren't telling the truth in 1996 when you requested to speak to a prosecutor? Isn't it true that you initiated the talks about the Samuels murder?"

"No, that is not correct."

"Isn't it true that you were in a jam — arrested for prostitution and drugs..."

"No, that's not true?" Maryann Settles shouted.

"Calm down, Mrs. Settles." The judge warned. "And let the government counsel finish his sentences."

"I'm sorry, your honor."

"Continue, Mr. McNeely."

"Thank you, your honor. Mrs. Settles, let me show you something. Your honor, what I have in my hand is the original affidavit that was submitted to defense counsel..."

"Original? What do you mean original?" The Judge asked.

"Your honor, the US Attorney's Office learned of the affidavit only days ago. I cannot account for its origin, but in the interest of justice, we ask that you view this document and then allow us to confront Mrs. Settles with it. So, there's no Brady violation, your honor..."

Jonathan Zucker rose from his seat. "Your honor, this would definitely be another Brady violation on the behalf of the government. The government has a duty to disclose all documents to include all BRUGLIO to the defense. Mr. McNeely just said that his office received this document days ago. That was more than enough time to disclose said documents to the defense..."

"I'm going to agree with Mr. Zucker, counselor. You cannot stonewall your Brady duty and then ambush this witness with it. Request denied, Mr. McNeely."

Ian McNeely looked like he suddenly had to take a shit. I smiled to myself, thinking about what Greg Gamble had tried to pull. He wanted McNeely to confront Maryann Settles with her original affidavit that had Susan Rosenthal in it. If he could point out the fact that the affidavit was amended, that did two things. It opened the door for the government to further portray Maryann Settles as a liar, given that the second affidavit omitted all talk about Susan Rosenthal and in the disposition and in court today. Maryann never mentioned that Susan Rosenthal had approached her for Greg Gamble. And it would have exposed Susan Rosenthal period. I never thought about the omission of Susan Rosenthal for too long. I noticed it, but never gave any of it that much thought. But now, I did, and my curiosity was thoroughly piqued. I made a mental note to talk to Maryann Settles before she left the court building. Glancing at my phone, I saw the missed calls. Two of them were from Quran.

Chapter 14
Greg Gamble

"Greg, we tried. Hamilton didn't go for it," Ian McNeely pleaded.

"There's no other way we can make Susan a part of this. You have to mention her when you take the stand. Once you do that, it's out there. Jonathan Zucker is going to put Maryann Settles on for a redirect. He has to. When he does, I'll be able to go into her affidavit and Susan further."

I paced the floor in the small room adjacent to the courtroom.

"We go back in, in about fifteen minutes. I'm going to go and grab a quick bite to eat. I'll see you when I get back."

As soon as the door closed, I smiled. Things were going just as I had predicted. And Ian McNeely said exactly what I knew he'd say. I sat in one of the chairs in the room to relax before it was time to perform. I thought about everything that had happened thus far. I thought about the certified mail I had received over the weekend that informed me that I was under investigation by the Office of Professional Responsibility and the Inspector General's Office. Those investigations were added on to the one I already knew about. The Department of Justice had informed me about their investigation and the General Accountability Office had also. Lines had already been drawn and sides taken. I knew that people in my office would be interviewed and past files, all closed over the last decade or so, would be reopened and scrutinized. Any case that had my name attached to it would be reviewed. Everybody with an ax to grind, every employee that I'd passed over for promotion, every unknown enemy would come to the light and thrust a dagger. It would be like Julius Caesar being assassinated by twenty daggers, thrusted by twenty different men. The media circus had revved up and intensified. I was a wounded surfer and all the sharks smelled blood in the water. I thought about the smug look that was plastered to Marg Roth's face as she stood outside the courtroom with her lackies. I smiled thinking about the future.

***

"Please state your name for the record."

"Gregory Gamble."

"Mr. Gamble, were you the United States Attorney in 1996?" Ian asked.

"No, I was not. I didn't become a US Attorney until a few years later. In 1996, I was an Assistant United States Attorney."

"Okay. I want to take you back to 1996, Mr. Gamble. Do you remember events that happened on January 17th, 1996?"

"I do. I was summoned by Susan Rosenthal and told that she had a woman in custody who wanted to talk about a murder that happened near her home. I was told the murder she wanted to talk about was a shooting on Sheridan Road where sixteen-year-old, Dontay Samuels was killed."

"Did you want to talk to the woman about the information she had?"

"Of course, I did. I was the prosecutor assigned to the Samuels case and since there was a man – Michael Carter in custody for killing Mr. Samuels, I wanted to hear what information the woman had."

"Do you recall who that woman was that wanted to talk about the Samuels murder?"

"Maryann Settles. That woman's name was Maryann Settles."

***

"Mr. Gamble, when were you told the name of the woman who wanted to talk about the Samuels case?"

"On the 17th of January 1996."

"Did you do any research on that woman?"

"Research?"

"Yes, research. Meaning — wait, let me ask the question better," Jonathan Zucker stated. "According to you, someone alerted you to a witness – a possible witness who had information she wanted to give about the Dontay Samuels murder, correct?"

"Correct."

"When did you find out that that witness was a woman?"

"In that same instance, I believe."

"Did you find out her name in that instance?"

"I don't recall. But maybe I did."

"Mr. Gamble, my question is important because what I'm asking is — once you learned that a possible witness — a woman wanted to talk, I need to know if you ran a check on the woman?"

"I think I did run a check that day, yes."

"Before or after meeting her?"

"Uh — I wanna say it was afterwards."

"I bet you would say that."

"Your honor, I object to that last response. Argumentative," Ian McNeely interjected.

"Sustained. Counselor Zucker, please keep unwarranted comments to yourself."

"Sorry, your honor. Mr. Gamble, you were alerted to the possibility of a witness, a woman who turned out to be Maryann Settles. You were alerted by Susan Rosenthal. Did you come to learn exactly how Susan Rosenthal had come across her info about Ms. Settles wanting to talk?"

"No, I don't recall that."

"Do you recall asking Mrs. Settles to lie..."

"I am a public servant. I never asked anyone to lie on anyone."

"So, it's your testimony, Mr. Gamble, that once you learned that Maryann Settles lived on Sheridan Road, right at the Dontay Samuels murder scene, that you never devised a scheme..."

"I never devised any schemes, Mr. Zucker."

"You never told Mrs. Settles to say that Michael Carter killed Dontay..."

"Maryann Settles came to us with that information. Maryann Settles wanted help with her charges. Maryann Settles said that she had witnessed the murder of Dontay Samuels on April 17th, 1995. Maryann Settles gave her information willingly. There was no coercion, no collusion, no deceit or agreement put forth by me to her to lie on anyone."

"So, Mr. Gamble, how do you explain the payments that were made to Mrs. Settles for an entire year?"

"It's not uncommon for my office to give witness vouchers to witnesses. The payments help with childcare, transportation, food — all types of expenses. It's been the practice of the United States Attorney's Office to give witnesses vouchers..."

"Vouchers, yes. But what about direct deposit payments to debit cards and cash payments, even after the witness has testified? Is that standard operating procedure for you and your office?"

"I can't say that it is. I personally never authorized or made any payments to Mrs. Settles or any other witness since I've been employed by the US Attorney's Office."

"But, you don't dispute the fact that those payments were made to Maryann Settles, correct?"

"Correct."

"Mr. Gamble, Maryann Settles testimony was essential to your case against Michael Carter, correct?"

"Essential, maybe. But we can't forget that there was another witness who also testified against Michael Carter. Maryann Settles was not the only witness."

Jon Zucker consulted some papers on the defense table, then he walked back towards the witness stand. "Oh, yes, Thomas Turner. Who's now deceased. Thomas Turner was not an eyewitness to the crime — to Dontay Samuel's murder, correct?"

"Correct."

"Thomas Turner was more of a hearsay witness, correct? A witness who claimed to appear on the scene after the shooting. He testified to a car leaving the scene. A man he identified as Michael Carter in the car and what he was told that happened that night. Is that about right?"

"It's been seventeen years, but it sounds about right."

"So, again, I ask you, was Maryann Settles the most essential witness at that trial?"

"I already admitted that she was essential."

"And let me ask you this, in your professional opinion, could Michael Carter have been convicted at trial WITHOUT Maryann Settles testimony?"

"There's no way that I can answer that question."

Chapter 15

Susan Rosenthal
United States District Court
300 Constitution Avenue NW
Washington, DC

"Your honor, it is widely held that the Sixth Amendment of the United States Constitution provides that in all criminal prosecutions, the accused shall enjoy the right to be confronted with witnesses against him. In Crawford versus Washington, the United States Supreme Court held that the Sixth Amendment guarantees a defendant's right to confront those who bear testimony against him. A witness's testimony against a defendant is thus inadmissible unless the witness appears at trial, or if the witness is unavailable, the defendant had a prior opportunity to cross examine. The question before this court today is whether or not the affidavits from a forensic analyst can be considered 'non testimonial'. In the case before you, Thomas Moore was charged and subsequently indicted for one count of trafficking cocaine. DC police received a tip that Thomas Moore, an employee at a public high school in the District was engaging in trafficking narcotics. The informant reported that Moore received numerous calls to his cell phone while at work and that on his lunch break everyday, he would be picked up in front of the school by a blue Mercedes Sedan. Minutes later, Moore would be returned to the school. DC police setup surveillance..."

***

"What happened?" Tabitha Kearney asked.

"The judge ruled that the admission of certificates at trial required the forensics analyst to testify in person. That the confrontation clause was violated in Moores trial because the certificates were 'testimonial' and the government was required to produce the analyst to be cross examined by defense counsel. So in essence, we lost. Thomas Moore wins. He'll be resentenced or have his conviction overturned outright and be released."

"Damn. you okay? I know how hard you worked on that motion to oppose Thomas Moore's conviction being overturned."

"I'm good, Tabitha. Have you been across the street and sat in on that Michael Carter hearing?"

"No, but it's still going on. We can head there now?"

***

DC Superior Court
501 Indiana Avenue NW

"Mrs. Settles, we needed to recall you to the stand to clarify a few things." Jon Zucker started. "On January 17th were you observed by law enforcement to be engaged in a public sex act?"

"Yes. An officer did observe that. He called out to us. I fixed my clothes and attempted to run away. When the officer caught up to me, he found drugs in my pocket."

"So, you do remember being charged with prostitution?"

"Vaguely, yes. At the police station, the only thing the police focused on was the drugs. Asking me questions about who sold drugs on Talbert Street and all this and that. Since I never went to court for the charges, I forgot about the prostitution charge."

"The prostitution charge disappeared, with..."

"Objection, your honor. Charges don't magically disappear." Ian McNeely said.

"It appears that these charges did just that, counselor McNeely. The witness said that she never went to court for any charges. It's reasonable to infer that her charges were dropped. Some may even say they disappeared. Please continue, Mr. Zucker."

"Thank you, your honor. Mrs. Settles, when you wrote the affidavit..."

"Which affidavit is he asking about, your honor?"

"Mr. McNeely, if you interrupt this examination one more time, I promise you, you'll spend all day tomorrow in a holding cell somewhere. Am I clear?"

"Yes, Your honor." Ian McNeely acquiesced.

"Mrs. Settles, when you wrote your affidavit, was your intention to hide anything about your prostitution charge?"

"No, sir. I didn't think it made any difference. I just wanted to be heard. wanted to try and right the wrong I committed at the behest of AUSA Greg Gamble. I was told to lie and say that Michael Carter killed Dontay Samuels. That I had witnessed him kill him. I agreed to lie at the grand jury session and in open court because I was afraid to go to prison back then. I was paid to lie on Michael Carter, but I didn't care about the money. I mean – I cared about it because it helped me continue to get high, but the money wasn't my motive for agreeing to lie. I didn't want to go to jail."

"I'm glad that you mentioned jail, Mrs. Settles. Are you aware of the fact that what you did in 1996 — lying under oath and implicating Michael Carter in a crime that he didn't commit, is considered perjury?"

Maryann Settles started to cry on the stand. I sat in the gallery seat and scowled, then smiled. I was sure that the woman's tears were fake.

"I'm aware of that, yes." Maryann Settles managed through her tears.

"And you still want to tell this court your story, correct?"

"Yes. I have to do the right thing. Even if I go to jail. I deserve to go to jail for what I did. I realize that now. That's why I came forward. Did the affidavit and sent it to Mr. Shankle. I knew that I can go to jail, but I'm not afraid of that anymore. I'm more afraid of what the Lord will do to me on my judgment day because of what I did. I know — well, I *knew* Michael Carter personally. He was always a fixture in the neighborhood. He's a few years younger than me, I believe, but I can still say that we grew up together. And he never did anything to me. To hurt me or otherwise and I feel terrible about what I did to him. Sending him to prison like that for something he didn't do. Michael Carter, I'm sorry, please..."

"Your honor, can you please direct the witness not to address the defendant in court. This is highly prejudicial to the government and I move to have this hearing..."

Judge Bruce Hamilton smiled. "You move to have the hearing, what, Mr. McNeely? Delayed? Stopped? Reheard? Or maybe you move for a mistrial? Because this hearing certainly has a trial feel to it but it's not a trial, Mr. McNeely. Mrs. Settles initiated this entire event when she recanted her trial testimony where she implicated Michael Carter as the person who killed Dontay Samuels. She's here today confessing to a crime that can send her to prison. I think she's entitled to tell the defendant personally that she's sorry for what she did. Continue, Mrs. Settles."

"I'm sorry for what I did. I apologize to Mr. Carter, to this court, to the taxpayers whose money was wasted. I apologize to the jurors that sat in on that trial in 1996. I lied to them and they believed me. I apologize to everybody affected by the lies I told in court in 1996."

"I have nothing further for this witness, your honor." Jon Zucker said.

"Make it quick, Mr. McNeely. We've been at this all day today and I'm ready to end this hearing."

"Mrs. Settles, you testified that initially you thought that the person was a lawyer, but you later learned that SHE wasn't? Correct?"

"Correct."

"When you said SHE, you were referring to a woman, correct?"

"I was, yes."

"And that woman took you to a different room and spoke to you, correct?"

"That's correct."

"Okay. Now, these payments that you were promised, you receive them, correct?"

"I received them, yes."

"Were any payments ever late?"

"Uh – I believe so, yes. Once or twice."

"And when those payments were late, did you contact someone about them?"

"Yes, I did."

"You contacted the person who arranged the payments?"

"Yes."

"Was that person Greg Gamble, Mrs. Settles?"

"No, it wasn't him.":

"Tell the court, Mrs. Settles, who the woman was that you spoke to initially. Who the woman was that introduced you to Greg Gamble. Tell us who the woman was that made the agreement to pay you. And who the woman was that you contacted when you didn't receive your payments. Was that woman the same woman in every instance I just named?"

"Yes, it was."

"And who was that woman, Mrs. Settles?"

"Susan Rosenthal."

"Greg Gamble, you sonofabitch!" I muttered to myself. I looked around the courtroom and saw Marg Roth now

IF YOU CROSS ME ONCE 5 | ANTHONY FIELDS

staring in my direction. Tabitha Kearney whispered something in my ear."

"Did you think that she would say something like that?"

Instead of replying, I stood up and hastily left the courtroom.

***

"I want him fuckin' dead!" I hissed into my cell phone after making sure that I was alone in the women's restroom on the first floor of the court building. "He's gone too far this time."

Carlos Trinidad's calm voice came through the line. "Are you fucking crazy? Don't ever call me from where you are saying things like that. When you finish work for the day, we'll meet up and talk then." The line went dead.

Taking a deep breath, I calmed myself down. At the sink, I splashed water all over my face. "This ain't too bad. You can come back from this. There's a perfectly good explanation for why you paid Maryann Settles. You just have to figure out what it is. I looked in the mirror at myself and blanched. Suddenly, I looked ten years older than I was. I could see crow's feet beginning to form in the corner of my eyes. I had frown lines embedded in the skin of my forehead.

Was I getting old right before my eyes? And why am I just noticing it? I shook my head to clear it of the cobwebs that covered doubt in my brain. Then suddenly, Greg Gamble's face came to mind. I'd seen him leaving the courtroom as I entered it, but we never acknowledged one another. Deep inside, I could sense that Greg knew what I was doing. And the stunt that Ian McNeely had just pulled in court had confirmed my suspicions. Now, with my name in the mix, there was no way I could come out of the fray untouched, unsoiled, unsullied. I slammed my palm down on the ceramic sink and shook my head. The initial conversation between me and Greg about the Maryann Settles situation came to mind...

I read the three page affidavit in its entirety before sitting in the chair in front of Greg's desk. The color drained from my face. I looked at Greg.

"Is this real?

Greg nodded. "Afraid it is. Gary Kolman copied it before passing it on to Jon Zucker. He gave me that copy today."

"She says that I made the payments to her."

"Susan, I know what it says."

"That happened sixteen, almost seventeen years ago."

"I know that."

"Well, what are we gonna do?"

"I don't know. But this can open Pandora's Box for us."

"For us? No. for you. That was standard operating procedure for you. Not for me. I only helped you with her. Maryann Settles. That one case. And I knew that I shouldn't have."

"So, says the woman who's been fucking and helping Carlos Trinidad for years. Don't fucking get up on your high horse on me, bitch! And don't look so surprised. Didn't think anybody knew, huh? Well, you thought wrong. One thing about me, Susan, is that I cover all the bases and I cover my ass. In 2003, when we indicted Kareemah 'Angel' El-Amin, DNA samples that matched the DNA taken from one of the murder victims was enough to go to trial. But, then you happened."

"Me? What the fuck do you mean, I happened?"

"You gave Carlos Trinidad's people Fatima Muhammad's location and got rid of the DNA samples. That's how Kareemah El-Amin beat the case."

"You can't prove that."

"You wanna bet?" Greg spat with venom.

"You can't be serious, right now."

"Does your husband Grant know any of your secrets, Susan?"

"Does anybody know yours, you fucking faggot? Or is that word politically incorrect these days? What do you like to be called these days, Greg? Queer?"

"It doesn't matter what you call me, Susan. Just remember to put 'boss' behind it."

"If you know that I'm in bed with Carlos Trinidad, you do know what he's capable of if his name comes up in this, right?"

"His name won't come up, if you don't want it to. Help me bury this situation with Maryann Settles and all of our secrets stay buried."

I could have just worked to bury the situation with Maryann Settles. There were ways to do it. Ways that could succeed without involving Carlos. But I had chosen to involve the drug kingpin and now look what happened? I thought back to the night I sat in Carlos's den and had drinks with him while we discussed Maryann Settles case. Carlos's words that night came rushing back to me with alarming clarity...

"Killing Maryann Settles and her husband is not the answer, Susan..."

"But, Carlos — you know — I've told you the damage this will..."

"Let me finish, chica. Listen to me. I just told you about my association to Michael Carter for a reason. As I said earlier, he didn't kill Dontay Samuels and I think it's time for him to be a free man. This affidavit situation with Maryann Settles recanting will facilitate him going free, number one. Number two, Greg Gamble has been and always will be a thorn in the men's side of my organization. I think it's time for him to go as US Attorney for the District of Columbia. It's time for you to take his place. You will be in the best possible decision to help yourself and my organization. It's your time. You've been at the US Attorney's office for almost twenty years. I'm going to have a talk with Maryann Settles and her husband. Things will proceed how they will, but you

will be taken completely out of the equation. There will be no mention of you anywhere. If this situation is as bad as you say it is, it should only cripple Greg Gamble and remove him from office. Once it takes full steam, you'll turn against him and advocate for him to be persecuted..."

Things hadn't went according to plan. "That shows how fucking smart you are, Carlos!" I said to myself and washed my hands. Greg Gamble had purposely dragged me into the scandal despite my carefully laid plans. Plan A had obviously failed. Now it was time for Plan B.

Chapter 16
Quran

"Where's your assistant?"

"Gone for the day." Zin replied.

"Are we going out to eat?"

"Later."

I sat in the chair by the wall in Zin's office and watched her move around with purpose. She faxed papers. Copied something. Pulled a book from the shelf that lined the wall, open it and flip the pages. I watched Zin read from the book and then replace it on the shelf. She bent over and looked for something on her laptop. "Want me to just come back later?"

"Quran, hush. Just sit there and be patient. I'm almost done."

I pulled out my cell phone and saw text messages from Tomasina, KiKi and Halima Ndugu. I suppressed my smile at seeing the text that Halima had sent. I was starting to think that she had ghosted me. After our last sexcapade, I'd heard exactly nothing from her. Calling her and getting no reply had dealt a blow to my self esteem. But only a tiny bit. I read their text messages and saw that I had two missed jail calls. Jihad and Dave. I made a mental note to get with Tom. I needed to get new phones to Dave and Jihad and some drugs. I didn't know if I should be upset or happy at the fact that I hadn't heard from Sean in like 4 days. I hadn't seen him since his breakdown in the Walmart parking garage. I couldn't stop thinking about the pain and heartache he was being crushed under due to the death of his daughter and his mother. I thought about the immense sadness I had felt when my mother died. It was as if I had lost the whole world. I imagined Sean's mother Sharon in life, happy and alive, and then imagined her putting a gun in her mouth and eating a bullet. I imagined someone ambushing Shontay and shuddered. I glance over at Zin, not yet showing any sign of pregnancy, but carrying my unborn child. Possibly a baby girl. I couldn't imagine having a child one day and then being childless the next day. I couldn't imagine the burden of guilt Sean had to hold in his shoulders knowing that his daughter had possibly died because of something he had done in the streets. Then I thought about all the sons and daughters I'd taken from their parents? All the lost souls I was responsible for separating from human bodies.

Then I remembered that most of the people I had killed were rodents. Vermin. Rats in human form. Most of them. But not all. I thought about Tony Wells. The man that Mike Carter tricked me into killing. I thought about Cindy Gamble. A woman who only wanted revenge for her brother Lonnell Gamble. A man that Sean killed for Mike Carter. I thought about Dontay. The best friend I'd killed just because he talked too much. I thought about my homie Mann; he had only wanted revenge for his niece Lands that I had killed. I thought about the woman I liked just because she was with Baby E, and about Javon Jarrett's brother. Gone from this world because his brother chose to stab Dave after Dave stabbed a pervert. Lastly, my mind settled on Tosheka; a woman I used to love and still cared about. A woman whose life I took as an abundance of caution. I killed Tosheka not for crimes that she had committed, but ones that she could possibly commit in the future. My heart strings tugged and I glanced up at Zin, who was busy pecking away on her laptop, now seated at her desk. Emotion threatened to take over me. Tosheka was my biggest regret. Not my blood brother Khitab, who'd dishonored the code. My biggest do over would be spent on Tosheka.

"There. That's about it." Zin announced and closed her laptop with a thud.

"All finished. Now, I can relieve some stress."

A sneaky smile crossed my face. "Relieve some stress, how?"

Zin moved from around the desk up to me. Before saying a word, she reached down, undid the straps on both YSL heels, then took them off. Her eyes on mine, Zin lifted her skirt and pulled down her panties. She unbuttoned her blouse until her breasts and stomach was visible. The clasp that held her large breast inside the bra was in the front middle. Zine undid the clasp and let the twins roam free.

I dropped my phone from my hand onto the floor.

"Stop acting like you don't know how I like to relieve stress." Zin said before bending over and unzipping my pants.

My dick sprung free and came immediately to life at her touch. Zin climbed into my lap and sat down on my hard on. She wiggled her breasts in my face. I grabbed her breasts and squeezed them together. My tongue darted out as if it had a mind of its own. I focused on one nipple as Zin grinded and rose on top of me.

"Damn... Quran... I needed... this!"

***

Union Market
1309 5th St. NE
Washington, DC

"They tried everything they could to portray Maryann Settles as a liar. And a whore. They brought up a prostitution charge that she didn't mention in the affidavit. Right tactic, wrong arena. That trick they pulled to besmirch that lady's character would've played well in front of a jury, but not in front of a judge. No matter what they tried, I think Maryann Settles was strong in her convictions, no pun intended. I think that she came across as truthful and penitent. She smiled, she cried, she got upset — she did good."

"Did Gamble get on the stand?" I asked.

"Yup. he got up there and lied. Tryna says that he never made no deal with Maryann and that she was paid witness vouchers to assist with transportation and shit like that. Childcare — the woman ain't even got no kids. He basically just did a good job of trying to save his ass. He threw Susan Rosenthal, his second in charge, under the bus. Jon did a decent job at cross examination. I think for some reason, he let Gamble off easy. Had it been me up there I would have lynched his ass."

I laughed at Zin. "Look at you. Pitbull in a skirt. Pretty as shit, sexy, smart, dangerous and vindictive. Helluva package."

Zin put her fork down and sipped her drink. "Glad you are acknowledging a real one. But you're about to have to add mother to that bundle. Pretty, sexy, smart, dangerous, vindictive mom. Think I like the sound of that."

I laughed again at a thought in my head.

"What's so funny. I want to laugh, too."

"You. I'm sitting right here thinking about the time when Gamble said that wild shit to you and had you twelve feet deep in your feelings. Remember that?"

Zin laughed. "Of course, I remember. That muthafucka told me he gon put me in my place. In the kitchen or a hip hop video. Told me that I was out of my league and said that shit about my father. I remember." Zin said and laughed even louder. "I wanted to kill that muthafucka. Had me mad as shit."

"Damn, that was a wild time, but I'm glad it happened."

"Glad it happened? Why would you say that?"

"Because your anger at Gamble gave you the heart to give me that ass. Remember that? That day you vented about what he said to you, you gave me that ass for the first time."

"I ain't gon lie. I forgot why I gave you some ass. Now, I'm glad that it happened, too, then. Because every now and then, I be needing to feel that dick back there. Shit hurt, but I can cum quick when you do it. Got me addicted to anal sex and shit. I'm a different woman because of you, Quran. Good and bad."

"Should I feel good or bad about that?" I asked.

"It don't matter. I'm yours and you're stuck with me."

"I'ma hold you to that."

"You do that. But, you bringing up the day that Greg Gamble said that shit about my father just made me remember something else."

"What?"

"Today, I met a world famous, black Attorney named J. Alexander Williams. Muthafucka looks like an older version of Shemar Moore. He is intelligent, crafty and renowned for his courtroom antics. They call him the new Johnny Cochran. Well, anyway, when I got to court, J. Alexander Williams was seated at the defense table with Jon Zucker. On one of the breaks, I spoke to him. He told me who he was and that he was there because a friend of my father had sent him. A very important friend. I thought about everything I knew about Jasper — that's what the J stands for — Jasper. I thought about everything I'd read or heard about Jasper Alexander Williams. I already told you that he's known all over the world for his skill at beating cases for the rich. I couldn't figure out who that person could be. Until just now. An article I read in the paper one day linked J. Alexander Williams to drug kingpin Carlos Trinidad. But I missed the connection until you just reminded me about what Greg Gamble said to me after the David Battle motion hearing."

"What else did he say to you?"

"He said, 'Behind the scenes, your father had people from the Trinidad organization try and intimidate witnesses. A few were killed. But in any fight where there's good versus evil, the good will always prevail. Now it all makes sense. In some shape or form, my father has been connected to the Carlos Trinidad organization. And I never knew it. J. Alexander Williams being at his hearing today proves that."

"Damn, your father must be a heavyweight of some kind. To be connected to niggas like Carlos Trinidad. He's got powerful friends..."

"Oh, do he?" Zin said and smirked.

"Yeah, I guess. Why do you say that like that? What's the smirk about?"

"You don't know anything about my father's friends and connections?"

I screwed my face up on agitation. "No. Why would I? How would I..."

Zin moved her plate of food from in front of her. She leaned in closer and said, "What we are about to do now is stop all the bullshit. It was cool months ago when we first started fucking. But now that we are officially a couple and we got a child on the way, we gon stop all the bullshit, Quran."

"Bullshit? What bullshit?"

"The bullshit you been feeding me for months now. I'm tired of the questions in my head. Either you gon tell me the truth..."

"About what? Tell you the truth about what?"

"Let me finish. You gon tell me the truth, Quran or I swear to God, I'ma get up and leave out this restaurant. And when I leave, it's gon be for good. I'm having this baby and raising this baby without you. I'm not playing with you. I stood by your side in an abandoned building and watched you kill your own brother. I proved to you that I could be trusted on every level. But all this lying you are doing is making me think that you don't trust me..."

"What lying am I doing? What the fuck...?"

"You keep lying about shit for no reason and that shit is throwing me off. Real bad! I been trying to keep cool..."

"Keep cool about what? Where is all this shit coming from?" I asked, genuinely perplexed. "I don't have a clue..."

"Let's go, Quran. Now. this ain't a conversation for the public."

Zin threw her napkin down, reached in her purse and pulled out cash.

"I got it." I said reaching in my pocket.

"Naw, I got it. I can pay for food." Zin replied and threw five twenty dollar bills down. "Let's go. Follow me to my condo."

***

Inside the Condo...

"You heard what I said in the restaurant, right? I meant every word of it. I don't know what the fuck it is with you and my father, but both of you are lying to me all the time..."

"Zin, I'm not lying..."

"See... you think I'm playing, don't you?" Zin said and stood up.

"You think I won't leave you, don't you?" She flashed a maniacal smile. "I'ma show you..."

"Sit back down, Zin, please." I pleaded. "Let's talk. I'll tell you whatever it is that you wanna know."

Zin sat back down across from me. "Why do you keep lying about you knowing my father? And please miss me with all that I know him from the hood like everybody else shit. I know all about the both of y'all. Why are you lying to me about him? He called your phone the other day. I answered your phone."

I decided that it was time to level with Zin. I tried to think about how much I'd tell her, but drew a blank. So, I just started talking. "Your aunt already told you about how close

111

my father and your father were. When my father got killed, I was lost. I was devastated, inconsolable. I never even thought about who may have killed my father or why it was done. One day, your father showed up and told me that I had to avenge my father and that he knew who killed him. Mike Carter took me to Wellington Park and showed me a dude named Tony Wells. He told me that Tony killed my father. I was twelve about to turn thirteen. I killed Tony Wells to avenge my father. But then Mike told me about a woman who was threatening him. He told me all about a dude named Lonnell Gamble that he made Sean Branch..."

"Sean Branch knows my father, too?"

I nodded.

"He never told me that. Ever."

"Your father introduced me to Sean after I killed Cindy Gamble."

"Wait — is — it can't be." Zin said over and over again.

I knew what Zin was thinking. I confirmed it by nodding my head.

"My father ordered the death of Greg Gamble's brother and his sister. Sean killed his brother and you killed his sister.

I nodded again. "And Greg Gamble knows that. How he knows is anybody's guess, but he knows. He told your father everything you just said when he got arrested for Dontay's murder. Greg Gamble told Mike that he paid the witness to lie and say Sean killed Raymond Watson to get Sean for killing his brother. He paid Maryann Settles to lie on your father because your father had his sister killed. And now he wants me in jail because he knows I killed his sister.

"Wait, wait, wait." Zin said as she stood up for the second time. She had removed her shoes and her skirt, but not the blouse. Zin's face was a mask of concentration. She paced the floor in the living room. "I can't believe it. So, that's why — now it all makes sense. Greg Gamble hates us all for a reason. I always knew that his actions — his words — were personal, but I was never sure. I went to see my father in

IF YOU CROSS ME ONCE 5 | ANTHONY FIELDS

Canaan before he came back to the city and I asked him did he know Greg Gamble before he got arrested. He looked me right in the face and lied. And I know he was lying. About Greg Gamble, about you, about a lot of shit. Now, it all makes sense." Zin walked until she stood directly in front of me. "So, let me ask you this. Greg Gamble knew that my father didn't kill Dontay Samuels. My father knew that he didn't do it. If he didn't do it, who killed Dontay Samuels?"

"I did." I admitted. "I killed Dontay."

Chapter 17
Zin

"I did. I killed Dontay."

Quran's truthful words were more digestible than the lemon peppered shrimp and pasta that I'd eaten at Union Market. To hear his admission was almost orgasmic for me. I knew that I was on the track that led toward a better understanding of a lot of things. "Why did you kill him? The two of you were best friends. Had grown up together, eaten together, slept in the same bed."

The look on Quran's face registered confusion. "How do you know that?"

"I'll explain after you. You first."

"I killed Dontay because your father told me to. Gave me an ultimatum. Either I killed Dontay or he would. Either way it went Dontay had been marked a dead man. Somebody told Mike that Dontay was saying that he killed his — he was saying a lot of shit that he wasn't supposed to say. Stuff about murders and shit that me, him and Mike had committed. Mike told me — asked me rather, did I wanna do thirty to forty years in jail because of Dontay's mouth. I decided that I didn't want to go to jail for a rack of years because Dontay talked too much. Instead of Mike killing Dontay, I told him that I would do it. Why? Because I had brought Dontay into the circle. I vouched for him when Mike asked if Dontay could be trusted. I was responsible for Dontay's actions." A single tear rolled down Quran's face. He wiped it away in a moment of vulnerability. "I was responsible for whatever mistakes he made. I knew that Dontay liked to brag. But I had no idea that he was bragging about murders and shit. Once it was decided that Dontay had to go, I knew that it had to be ME who did it, not Mike Carter. Days after it was decided, we rode past — I was in the car with Mike; the 500 SL he had back then. Dontay was on his mother's porch. I walked up and shot him. Then I walked back to the Benz and got in the car with Mike. Later, when he was arrested for murder, I didn't understand why. Mike never told me the whole entire story until he got to Lorton and I went to visit. But before and during his trial, I hunted T.T. and Mary..."

"T.T.?"

"Thomas Turner. He was a crackhead from down the street near Pomeroy Road. I knew his brothers Anthony and Earl and his two sisters, Robin and Sandy. He got locked up on a rape beef and beat it. He beat it because Gamble gave him immunity to tell on Mike. I looked for both of their asses to kill them, but the feds had them hidden somewhere. Even when they appeared in court during Mike's trial, they were protected. When he got convicted, I felt like it was all my fault. That's when Mike summoned me to Lorton and he told me everything. Admitted everything to me about his beef with the Gamble family."

I walked around the living room thinking about everything Quran said. Then my conversation with my father in Canaan's visiting hall came to mind...

"Jonathan Zucker believes that not only does this free you, it creates a scandal at the US Attorney's office that Greg Gamble can't stand up under."

"Fuck Greg Gamble and his whole family."

"Speaking of Greg Gamble, do you know him personally?"

"Personally? What do you mean personally? He was the prosecutor on my case."

115

"I mean, did you know him before you got locked up? I ask because all this shit with him seems personal..."

It was as if I could hear his voice inside my head. All I had to do was listen.

"Fuck Greg Gamble. I could have been..."

"Dad, you could've been what? What were you gonna say just now?"

"Nothing, baby. Forget it. Don't pay that coward no mind. He's just mad because I..."

"When Greg Gamble said that you had people from the Trinidad Organization trying to intimidate witnesses and what he said about witnesses getting killed..."

"He lied. If that was the case, why were the remaining two allowed to live to testify? He was just tryna rattle your cage. And speaking of the two witnesses, if Maryann Settles has recanted, they still have Thomas Turner. What about that?"

"Good question. I'm not exactly sure how that works. You gotta ask Jon Zucker that question."

"Cool. I will. But back to your original question. Did I know Greg Gamble before I got charged with Dontay Samuel's murder? The answer is no. Never met him until he got assigned to prosecute my case..."

"I knew his ass was lying."

"Who?"

"My father. When I asked him did he know Greg Gamble personally before he got arrested. I told him that the whole situation had a personal feel to it. After all the wild shit that Gamble said to me about my father at the court building. He looked me right in my face and lied. About everything. Which brings me back to you. Why did you lie to me about knowing my father? You never answered that?"

"And you never answered my question, either. How did you know about me and Dontay being best friends?"

"Why have you lied about your relationship with my father for all this time?"

"Because," Quran started and looked away from me. "It was easier to lie. How was I supposed to tell you that I killed people for your father? That he called me and gave me info on rats and paid me to kill them? How could I tell you about our past and still expect you to love me the same. When you first asked me about your father, I was still trying to get you to love me. I couldn't tell you the truth."

"The truth?" I repeated and chuckled. I paced the floor a few more times before coming back to the loveseat and sitting down across from the couch that Quran sat on. I looked at Quran as if I could see straight through his rugged good looks, Hugo Boss attire and butter Gucci boots. "Have you told me the truth, Quran?"

"Yeah."

"The whole truth?"

"What do you mean by that?"

"Who killed my mother Quran?"

"What?"

"Scratch that. Let me push the restart button. Did you know my mother, Quran?"

"I – I – no – not like that. Naw."

"You didn't know my mother?"

"I met her before, but I didn't — I wasn't around her enough to say that I knew her."

"But you had met her before, right?"

"Yeah."

"And you saw her on more than one occasion, right?"

"Zin," Quran asked, suddenly rattled, "Where are you going with this?"

"Where I just was moments ago. Did you kill my mother?"

Quran leapt to his feet. "Hell no! Fuck I'ma kill your mother for?"

"I'ma ask you this, Quran and I want you to be very mindful of your reply. Because the way you answer this question may dictate whether or not we have a future. And do me a favor and sit back down."

"Man — you on some bullshit, Zin!"

"Quran, sit the fuck down!" I demanded.

Shaking his head, Quran finally complied and sat down.

"Did Dontay Samuels beat, rape and kill my mother?"

"Fuck no!" Quran answered with conviction.

"Did you beat rape and kill my mother?"

"Hell — fuckin — No! Why would you ask me — why would you even think some shit like that?"

I got up from my seat and crossed the room until I found my purse. I fished inside the purse until I found my mother's letter. I took the letter to Quran and gave it to him. "Read that."

"What the fuck is this?"

"Read it."

Quran unfolded the pages of the letter and started to read.

I sat quietly on the opposite couch and let him read the entire letter.

Quran's silence after reading the letter spoke volumes.

"I'ma ask you again. Did you beat, rape and kill my mother, Quran? Tell me the truth. If you want us to have a future, tell me the truth."

"Your mother believed that Mike killed my father."

"Did you beat, rape and kill my mother?"

Quran shook his head. "No. I didn't kill your mother. And neither did Dontay."

"Who beat, raped and killed my mother, Quran?"

"Your father did. Mike did all that shit."

"My father killed my mother?"

Quran nodded. "Yeah. You gotta believe me, Zin. I swear by Allah that we didn't do it. Your father called Dontay and told Dontay to pick me up. He did. When we got to y'all house, your mother was dead. Please, baby, you gotta believe me."

Tears welled up in my eyes and fell. I tried to wipe them away but they were quickly replaced with new ones. "I believe you, Quran. Earlier, you asked me how I knew that you and Dontay were best friends and so forth. I knew that because I met Dontay's mother Delores a few weeks ago and she told me everything. Dontay told his mother exactly what you just said. That my father called him one day and told him to pick you up and that y'all went to my parents house. He told her that when y'all got there, my mother was dead. He told her that the two of you helped my father move my mother's body."

"Zin — I'm sorry! I was..."

"A kid. I know that, Quran. A fourteen year old who did whatever my father told him to do. I'm not mad at you about that. I was initially, but I thought about it long and hard after I learned that you did that and I decided to forgive you. Besides, your crime that day was a lesser crime than what I originally thought when I first found that letter in my mother's things at the condo. I've known for a while now that my father killed my mother. I guess I just wanted to hear it from you. I had to hear it from you. So, let me ask you this question. After reading that letter, how do you feel about my father now?"

"Different. He was like a father to me. Now, I want to kill him."

Chapter 18
Susan Rosenthal

"In the news tonight, today's top story is United States Attorney Gregory Gamble appearing in the court to refute allegations that he bribed and coerced a witness to falsely implicate a DC man in a murder trial seventeen years ago. Michael Carter was in court today for an evidentiary hearing that lasted several hours. A female witness took the stand and admitted to committing perjury in Michael Carter's trial in 1996. The witness told a judge that she was arrested two blocks away from where Dontay Smauels was killed January 17th 1995. She alleges that due to her home address being right at the scene of that murder, she was chosen by Greg Gamble and his second in command Susan Rosenthal to say that Michael Carter committed the murder. The witness now says that she wasn't in the DC area on the night of the murder and only claimed to be because she was coerced, bribed and paid by Greg Gamble and Susan Rosenthal..."

Carlos clicked a button near his seat and the large screen TV in his den went blank. He picked up a glass and sipped from it.

I was livid. Everything that was happening is what I was trying to avoid. Marg Roth spoke first. "Sue, I'm sorry that your name came up in all of this, but this was your baby. You asked me to make this hearing and Greg Gamble a major focus of the news. I only did what you asked. I control Gannet and people at Eyewitness News 9. I can't control the

Washington Post and other news agencies. *Fox News* is all Rupert Murdoch. Besides, you saw how many other media people and news outlets were in the courtroom. Don't blame me..."

"I don't blame you." I told Mary Roth then turned to face Carlos. "I blame you."

Carlos Trinidad smirked and then laughed. 'You blame me?"

I got up from my seat and walked close to Carlos. "I came to you, Carlos and I told you the entire situation. I told you that under no circumstances could I be implicated in this mess. I told you that if my name came up, the scandal would cast me out and cost me everything. I told you about the voucher stubs that would strengthen Maryann Settles's allegations. In order to keep my position at the US Attorney's office and continue to help you as I always have, I needed the past to stay buried."

"You asked me to have Maryann Settles and her husband killed."

"To make this whole mess go away. Without her, there was nothing but a useless affidavit. Her allegations in it would have fallen on deaf ears and been forgotten about in weeks. But you chose some ridiculous loyalty to Michael Carter and some dead guy named Ameen Bashir..."

"I made her change the affidavit. She removed you..."

"But that wasn't enough, Carlos! I knew that it wouldn't be. You don't know Greg Gamble like I do. He's a shifty, crafty muthafucker. A highly intelligent man who sees all the angles, plays all the angles. He manipulated us. He used Ian McNeely like a puppet. You thought that getting Maryann Settles to rewrite her affidavit, that that would be enough to shield me. Gamble saw both affidavits. He picked up immediately on the fact that I was omitted from the newest one. He plate coy and slow, but he knew exactly what he would do when it was time to perform. And he did it. He got right on that stand and complicated ME! Once the lid was off the can, it couldn't be put back on. You said that you wanted me at the helm. In the top spot at 555 4th Street. Well, guess what? That's not going to happen now. Why? Because you didn't FUCKING LISTEN TO ME!!"

"Since you put it like that, I guess I'm at fault. I underestimated Greg Gamble. Never again will I make such a mistake. But I don't see things as being as bad as you think. You will survive this scandal. Greg Gamble won't. Trust me on that. Benito?" Carlos called out to his trusted companion and oldest friend.

"Yes, mi amigo?" Benito appeared and said.

"Set up a meeting with Ross at the Department of Justice and Burt Ryans at OPR. Then I need you to send Macro to Brandywine, Maryland. Get rid of the Settles for me, please and I need to know everything I can about US Attorney Greg Gamble."

"Now, I need a drink." I announced.

Dorothy Benigan, the US Marshal woman in Carlos's employ, walked over to the bar and mixed a drink. She poured the mixed drink into two cups. She walked over to Marg Roth and handed her one. The other came to me.

I sipped the fruity concoction. "Margaritas make me lascivious." I said and finished the liquor in three gulps. "Real Lascivious."

***

Sex with Carlos was never dull. He was a master at the art of seduction. His tongue skillfully surveyed every inch of my sex. Sitting in the chair in his den, my legs askew to allow him a perfect access to me, I gripped Carlos's head and ran my fingers through the salt and pepper unruly curls. I could feel the excess wetness of my pussy as juices mixed with his saliva ran down my inner thighs. I opened my eyes and spied on Dorothy and Marg. The two beautiful women were in the 69 position on the couch across from where I sat. I became a voyeur. I couldn't take my eyes off of Marg Roth. In her late thirties, Marg resembled Carmen Diaz. her skin had a tanned hue, her body athletic and toned. The sparkle of the diamonds in the anklet around her leg drew my eyes to the tattoo on her foot and pedicured toes. I watched attentively as her toes curled in rhythm to Dorothy's oral assault on her pussy. Moans escaped my mouth as I neared a powerful orgasm. The look on Marg's face was hidden to me, but I knew that it mirrored my own. I knew from experience that no matter how good you ate Dorothy, she'd never stop her methodical assault on the pussy she tongued. Just as a tinge of jealousy crept into my core, I gripped Carlos's head and gave him my essence.

Chapter 19
Sean Branch

The kid was totally unaware of my presence on the side of the house. Staking out the Best home on Mills Avenue was painstaking, but necessary. There were so many people who came and went inside the house that I couldn't keep track of everybody. But I could keep track of the kid. I called him the kid, but the young dude that approached the house now had to be a teenager about fourteen or fifteen years old. He was dressed in a black Helly Hanson snow suit to ward off the extreme cold, black foamposite sneakers and a Helly Hanson hat that was pulled down over his shoulder length dreads. I'd watched him leave the house on the hill an hour ago. I didn't have to follow him because I knew exactly where he was headed. The store on the corner near Rhode Island Avenue was his destination, then the carry out next door. It was where the young dude went every night before going in for the night. Although I'd grown up with certain members of the Best family, I didn't know the kid. Couldn't know him. He'd been born while I was in prison. He was now a couple yards away. I leapt out of my hiding spot with the suppressed four fifth aimed at his face.

"What the...?" The kid exclaimed.

I walked closer to him until I was inches away. "I'ma ask you a couple questions, youngin'. If you lie you die. Do I make myself clear?"

The kid nodded.

"What's your name?"

"K-K-Kendrick?"

"Are you a Best, Kendrick?"

He nodded again.

"How? Who's your mother or father?" I asked him.

"My mother is Charmaine." The kid answered.

"Charmaine Best? She's the youngest Best sister. So, Kenny and Jew Bey, your uncles?"

The kid nodded.

"I'ma friend of the family, but I need to make sure that your family is still friends of mine. Somebody killed your uncle Moe recently, right?"

"Y – Yeah."

"Who does your family think did it? Who do they think killed Moe?"

"Um — I — they don't know who it was, but somebody told my grandmother that a dude named Sean Branch did it."

"Is that right?"

"How many people in the house right now?"

The kid hesitated to speak.

"Talk or die. And don't lie."

"Uh — just my grandmother, my mother, sister and my uncle Gerald."

"Where is Jew Bey and Kenny?"

"They ain't here. They don't live here."

"Where do they live?"

"I — I don't know."

"Wrong answer, youngin'." I said and shot the kid in the face. His body dropped. I shot him again, then dragged him into the brush on the side of the house. In his pockets I found the keys to the house. It took me a minute to find the right keys to fit the lock,, but eventually, I did. I walked into the dimly lit house through the side door.

"Kendrick, is that you? Bring me my damn cigarettes!" A woman shouted from upstairs. "Kendrick? You hear me, boy?"

I walked through the side foyer into the living room. On a couch laid a teenage girl watching television. She looked up as I approached. She sat up and before she could make a sound, I shot her. The house was junky as shit and smelled bad. I moved through the rest of the house in search of the other two women and the one man, Moe's youngest brother Gerald. I'd been in the Best home before and remembered the layout. Off the kitchen, there was a basement that doubled as a bedroom. I decided to go there first. Finding the door that led to the basement was easy. Descending the stairs quietly was harder. Gun in hand, I reached the basement and sure enough, on an air mattress in the middle of the room laid, Gerald Best. he never moved as I approached. He was asleep. I shot Gerald in the head twice. When I got back to the kitchen, a woman was there. Her back to me, she rummaged inside the refrigerator.

"Hey," I whispered, startling her.

The woman turned around to face me. It was Charmaine Best.

"Sean?"

I nodded. "I need you to call Kenny for me, Charmaine."

"What? What's going on? Why..."

"Wrong answer, Charmaine." I replied and shot her repeatedly in the face and body.

"These muthafuckas can't answer simple questions." I muttered as I left the kitchen. Mildred Best was the matriarch of the entire Best clan. I stopped on the stairs that led upstairs and thought about all the things that she'd done for me when I was a kid. I thought about the icy cups that she gave out and all the cake and pies. I thought about the halloween and Thanksgivings I'd shared in the house. The candy apples and fried chicken. The Easter egg hunts in her backyard and me trying to dry hump the other two Best girls. A voice in my head begged me to just leave the house. To spare Mrs. Mildred Best. But I couldn't I wouldn't. I went back down the steps and entered the kitchen. I found a good knife in seconds. If I had a heart, I'd leave without any further bloodshed. But, I didn't have a heart. It died with my daughter.

***

The smell of fresh blood was alluring to me. I saw the blood seep from the pillowcase and saturated the upholstery inside the van on the floor. I tried to figure out why I decided to take Mildred Best's head and couldn't. The spur of the moment decision couldn't be explained. But the message it sent the remaining Best children and grandchildren would say everything that I could not. There would be a time of great mourning for the family. I thought about the five lost souls back in Mills Avenue and shook my head. Collateral damage. I drove around the streets of DC until I found a place to pullover and rest. I glanced over at the pillowcase that contained Mildred Best's head. I reached over and grabbed it. Reaching inside, I pulled out the head. The old women's eyes were open. "Stop looking at me." I said and laughed. Then I propped the head up in the van's passenger seat. I didn't feel like being alone. I thought about all the people I'd killed in the last five days. I hoped that people didn't think I was finished. Because little did the world know, I was just getting started.

Chapter 20

Detective Bob Mathis
1800 blk of Mills Avenue
Northeast, DC
2:37 a.m.

Police work seemed to never stop. Sleep had taken me for a couple of hours before I got the call. Five people dead. Two males and three females. All relatives of Maurice 'Moe' Best. I pulled my car near the yellow tape that cordoned off the top of Mills Avenue. The house on the hill was one that I knew well. I'd sat in front of it with Moe Best on too many occasions to count as he told me everything about drug trafficking, guns and wars in the Langdon Park, Montana area. Because of the slain confidential information, countless murders had been solved. So, I owed it to him to bring his family's murderer to justice. As soon as I opened the car door, my ears were bombarded with screams and wails. Law enforcement and crime scene technicians scoured the outside and inside of the house on the hill. Throngs of people gathered in the cold to mourn the deaths, the murders of the Best family. I could pick out the relatives of the dead by those who cried the hardest and wailed the loudest. Two men sat on the curb near the yellow tape. Both broken in grief surrounded by others who attempted to console them. I recognized both men. Kenneth Best and Jeremy 'Jew Bey' Best. I ducked under the yellow tape and zipped my Northface parka up to the neck to ward off the chill.

"Bob," Det. Thomas Huff said as I approached.

"Tom. walk me through it." I said.

Tom Huff led me up the front steps and into the gate that surrounded the house. "We found one body here. A teenager. ID'ed as Kendrick Best, fifteen years old. Student at Hamilton Career Center on Mt. Olive Road. born and raised here in this neighborhood. In this house. We believe he was ambushed as he walked up to the house. Over there on the ground is a bag he was carrying. Actually, he carried two. Cigarettes and candy in one bag. Chinese take-out in the other. The killer or killers took his keys and entered the house. Kendricks sister, Kalima was killed in the living room on the couch. She was thirteen years old. In the kitchen, we found a body on the floor. A woman. Shot repeatedly in the face and body.

Turns out, she's Charmaine Best, Kendrick and Kalima's mother. In the basement, there's another body. That victim is ID'ed as Gerald Best, thirty years old, worked at the Wharf on a boat called Captain Jock's. Shucked oysters, scaled fish, that sort of thing. Lastly, in an upstairs bedroom, there's another body. Believed to be Mildred Jean Best, seventy years old, retired, owner of the house, mother and grandmother to the rest of the deceased..."

"Believed to be? She hasn't been ID'ed?"

Tom Huff paused. He spit out the tobacco he was sucking on. After putting a fresh wad of Skoal chew in his mouth, he said, "Couldn't ID her, Bob. The fucker that killed her cut off her head. And took it with him. Or her. The fucking head is nowhere to be found."

I could only think of three words to say. "Fuckin' Sean Branch."

***

Four hours later...
Violent Crimes Branch

Pennsylvania and Branch Avenue

The coffee in the station tasted like warm shit turds ground into coffee beans. I pushed the styrofoam cup away from me. "Have crime scene search to scour every surface in that house. Get every fingerprint they can so that we can cross match them with the ones we have for Sean Branch."

"Bob, how can you be so sure that the killer was Sean Branch?" Tom Huff asked. "All of the Best son's were in the streets."

"Not Gerald. He was different. That's all Moe Best used to say about his younger brother. He wanted to protect him. And the rest of the family."

"Well, that didn't go too well, did it?" Det. Joe Anastasia said.

"Listen to this, though. Apparently there's a slight connection going on here. In the midst of all of this madness. The house on Decatur Street that appeared to just blow up with Damien Tyler inside of it wasn't — well, it was blown up, but not on its own like some of us originally suspected freak accident, I said. Something electrical or maybe a gas furnace blew." Joe Anastasia shook his head. "ATF crime scene people found remnants of what they believe was a hand grenade..."

Jake Reese chuckled. "Hand grenades? So, we're dealing with street thugs and killers with hand grenades now?"

"Hey, I'm just passing on what ATF told me. But, that is not the gist of my story. The house in Ivy City belonged to Dorenda Tyler. Does that name ring a bell to anyone present over forty years old?" Nobody spoke up. "Dorenda Tyler was the wife of Van Tyler."

"Now, that name I remember." Tom Huff commented. "Von Tyler was Wayne Perry before there was a Wayne Perry. Allegedly killed a lot of people in Northeast. Said to have single handedly started the Ivy City/Trinidad neighborhood beef in the early eighties. Every other few days bodies were popping up. Shit lasted until the late nineties. And now that I think about it, his wife Dorenda was also implicated, but never charged with any murders. Haven't heard her name in years."

Det. Joe Anastasia nodded. "In history class you must've gotten all good grades. Well, Sherlock, here's a puzzle that needs solving. Dorenda Tyler has been on the straight and narrow since Von Tyler was killed. She's working at a hospital downtown somewhere. I went to the blast site on Decatur Street and encountered her. Damien Tyler was her nephew. I learned a little about him from her. According to her, he was a good kid that recently came to live with her. He wanted to get away from the environment he lived in in Ward eight. No enemies that she knew of and no reason that anyone would want to hurt him. Asked her if she knew any reason why someone would want to bomb her house. Someone from the past maybe. She claimed to have no known enemies, either. The way things played out tells me that whoever tossed the grenade into the house wanted someone to run out. Damien Tyler was shot after he came out of the house. He was targeted, but may not have been the target. So, I go on to question Dorenda Tyler and I learn that her and Von Tyler produced one child. A daughter. Further questioning revealed that the daughter's name is Renaissance Tyler. Okay, stay with me now. Almost two months ago, three men got shot on Orleans Place in Northeast..."

"Miguel Harris and Deontay Wilks were killed. Jontavious Minor survived that shooting. He talked to me and Rio Jefferson at the hospital. According to him, Miguel Harris was talking to Crud's brother, Brion about Crud getting killed. At some point the conversation went left and threats were made. Brion left. Minutes later, a woman appeared and started shooting. On Orleans Place, we talked to possible witnesses to the shooting. No one wanted to get involved in the case, but one person did identify the woman who may have been the shooter. The witness called the woman Ren and said that she was from Ivy City." Jake Reese added.

"You just stole my thunder, Jake," Joe Anastasia said before continuing. "Renaissance Tyler goes by the name Ren and was the girlfriend of Brion Clark..."

"Ren Tyler was at Stewart's funeral home with Brion Clark the evening he was killed." Nate Hackett said.

"So, does anybody here believe that it's a coincidence that Bionca Clark was shot and killed on her porch and then hours later, Ren Tyler's house was bombed and her cousin Damien killed?"

"Sounds like good detective work, Joe and I'm proud of it, but Bionca Clark wasn't killed on the porch of her mother's house." I flipped through the pages of my notebook. The woman killed on that porch was thirty year old Celine James. We have been looking for Bionca Clark, but there's no sign of her thus far. I believe that you're onto something, though, so keep at it. Get a full background check on Renaissance Tyler. Daughter might've picked up the killing gene from her mom and dad. Somebody do a full check in Bionca Clark, too. I just had a thought. Jake, do you have the video footage from outside the Chipotle on the night of Shontay Dunn's murder, yet?"

"Not yet," Jake Reese replied, "but I should have it soon."

"Good, because as soon as you get it, let me know. And there's one more thing that's been bothering me. When the six people got shot and killed in the building on Hayes Street, nobody reported hearing any gunshots. At the Best house earlier, the same thing. There are houses that neighbor both sides of it, yet no one heard any gunshots..."

"And now that you mention it, nobody on Decatur Street heard Damien Tyler getting shot, either. They heard the blast and saw Damien Tyler on the ground suffering from gunshot wounds." Joe Anastasia said.

"Wait a minute guys," Jake Reese interjected. "Are you implying that we're dealing with a serial killer who has hand grenades and silencers?"

Det. Matt Arnold, who'd been relatively silent all night, cleared his throat and said, "Before you answer that question, before anyone answers that question, there's something else. I have been in constant communication with Jacob Newsome, the detective investigating the quadruple homicide at the Woodmore Town Center. As we all know, three of the victims in that case — well, the three male victims were a part of a drug gang in Clay Terrace. The feds were investigating two of the three men. The lone female victim's name was Antriece Fortune. Antrice Fortune's father was killed a few weeks ago..."

"Tony Fortune?" Phil Krouse asked.

"Yes. him. Tony Fortune. Two days ago, his other daughter who was there at the scene in Prince George's County but was not injured that night, was shot and killed near Lincoln Heights on 51st Street. And just like Bob just said, there were no gunshots heard."

"What was the victim on 51st Street's name?" I asked.

"Antoinette Fortune."

"Was she a witness in the quadruple case?"

"No. Jacob Newsome said she wouldn't talk." Matt Arnold replied. "They talked once. She said that her father would kill her if she talked to the police."

"And now they're both dead. I'm starting to hear the words 'connection' again. In most of the recent murder cases. Everybody keep up the good work. I think I need to talk to Greg Gamble again. I need to hear those recordings again."

Chapter 21
Greg Gamble

I realized at a young age that I was different from the other boys I knew. I wasn't real athletic. I didn't like remote control cars, vibrating football games, video games or sports. I didn't like playing tag or any of the other games that kids played in the projects. I didn't like girls, or dolls, easy bake ovens or jumping rope or make up. Outside of my family members, I didn't like it very much at all. I was introverted and inquisitive. I like jigsaw puzzles, the rubik's cube and anything that challenged my mind. I would break all of my toys just to see how they worked. Once broken, I labored to put them back together again. Sometimes I succeeded, but oftentimes I failed. I hated failure. I promised myself as a kid that when I grew up, my failures would be few and my successes would be many. I pulled out the recordings from the device that was planted in David Battles cell at CTF and put the thumb dime into my computer. There were hours of listening to do, so I put my earbuds in and got to it.

***

The next morning...
U.S. Attorney's Office
555 4th St. N.W.
"There's someone here that you need to listen to, Greg." Tabitha Keerney said. "I'm prosecuting his case and he's

decided to talk to us to avoid a lengthy prison sentence. He's been talking about a lot of things, but there's a certain area in particular that I think you'll like what you hear."

"Who is this guy, Tabitha?" I asked.

"His name is Joshua Clark and he's in jail for statutory rape. He's thirty years old and he has a predilection for sixteen years olds. It's his second charge of this nature. He knows he can't go back to prison for this charge again so he wants to bargain."

"And you think he has information that I want to hear?"

Tabitha nodded. "Trust me, you're going to be glad that I came to you with this."

"Where is he now?"

"Downstairs in one of the interview rooms. He's being held at the DC jail in a max housing unit. He wants out of there. I want to move him to either Warsaw or Piedmont in Farmville, Virginia. But only after I get the okay from you."

"Okay, Tabitha, my curiosity is piqued. Take me to him."

***

"Joshua, this is my boss, United States Attorney Greg Gamble. He's the one who makes all the decisions in this building. I've told him what you want and about how you intend to help us, now and in the future." Tabitha Kearney said. "You have talked to me and you've spoken to my colleague Devin York, but I need you to talk to my boss. He's going to listen to you and he may ask some questions. Be sure to answer all of his questions openly and honestly, okay?"

"Okay." Joshua Clark replied.

"Now, you've told me and Devin lots of things, but what I'm particularly interested in right now is the murder of your friend James Yarborough who was killed on Half Street in Southwest last month. But before you get into that, go back to the beginning and tell the whole story."

135

"Aight. My man Doo Doo is from my neighborhood..."

"Joshua, who is Doo Doo?" Tabitha asked.

"Oh, my bad. Doo Doo is James Yarborough. We call him Doo Doo in the hood."

"Okay. Please continue."

"Doo Doo hung with three dudes that I knew of all the time. Whistle, Crud and Miguel. A couple months ago, Doo Doo told me that some niggas — I mean, some dudes had a hit out on Crud. Something about Crud snitching on a dude named Buck from MLK. Doo Doo was in prison with a dude named Sean Branch..."

I was familiar with all the names that the man was saying because they were all recently dead, killed in the streets, but when he mentioned the name Sean Branch, I knew exactly why Tabitha had come to fetch me. I was wide eyed and one hundred percent attentive suddenly.

"Sean Branch paid Doo Doo to set up Crud. Just Crud. And Whistle helped him do it."

"Why would Doo Doo and Whistle agree to set up Crud for Sean Branch?" I asked. "If they — Doo Doo, Crud and Whistle, were friends?"

"Crud didn't get a name like Crud for no reason. He was a dirty, grimy, dope fiend ass nig... dude. Doo Doo was friends with him and Whistle, but he knew how cruddy they both were. He wouldn't have agreed to set Crud up for free, he did it to collect the money that was on Crud's head."

"Who put up the money on Crud's head? Do you know?"

Joshua Clark shook his head. "Naw, I don't know that."

"And Doo Doo never said?"

"Naw. All he told me was that he was paid to get Crud somewhere so that Sean Branch could kill him. He enlisted Whistle and they lured Crud to Penny's house on -"

"Third Street in Southeast."

Joshua nodded. "Him and Whistle jumped on Crud and tied him up. Later that day, Doo Doo said that two dudes came to the house. Sean Branch and a dude Sean called Quran..."

I leaned forward in my seat. The story was getting better and better.

"Sean Branch killed Crud and cut his head off. The other dude with him killed Whistle..."

"The other dude — the one that Sean called Quran killed Whistle?" I asked.

"Yeah. Doo Doo said that Sean and the dude Quran said that Whistle was hot, too. That he had snitched on the same case. The one from MLK. On Buck and some other dudes. After Whistle and Crud were dead — he said that Sean Branch put Crud's head in a pillowcase and took it with him — Sean told him to set the house on fire. Which he did, but it didn't burn all the way up. Days later, we were around the way gambling..."

"Around the way? Around what way?"

"We were gambling on the sidewalk on Langston Lane. I'm from Woodland for real, for real, and our hoods, the Lane and Woodland usually be beefing, but for the last couple of years, we been together going at them Bang Bang niggas."

"Bang Bang?"

"Yeah. That's what them Harford Street nig — dudes call themselves. Anyway, me, Doo Doo and some more niggas from the Lane were outside gambling when this silver Lexus pulls up. A dude gets out of the car. Since the Lane does a lot of beefing with other dudes' hoods, everybody stopped gambling to focus on the dude in the Lexus. Doo Doo knew the dude. Called him Blast...

"Blast is Brion Clark, Crud's brother. Speaking of which, your name is Joshua Clark. Are you any relation to those Clarks, Brion and Crud. and don't lie. We'll know if you are."

"Fuck no, I ain't no kin to them niggas. I ain't even know their last name was Clark. I knew Crud from Doo Doo, that's it. So, the dude Blast was Crud's brother?"

IF YOU CROSS ME ONCE 5 | ANTHONY FIELDS

I nodded.

"Damn," Joshua Clark exclaimed, "Now, it all makes sense. The dude in the silver Lexus named Blast talked to Doo Doo for a few minutes on the Lane and then Doo Doo came back to the crap game. He won some money and then lost it back. After that, he hopped in the car with the dude he called Blast.

Doo Doo had just copped the Cadillac CTS-V wagon and all he did was brag about it. So, him not driving it was the first red flag to me. The second one was when the silver Lexus pulled off the Lane, a red Infiniti truck that had been sitting idle with a bitch – I mean woman in it, pulled off behind them and seemed to follow them. I filed the red flags and kept it moving. When Doo Doo never came back for his car, I knew that something was wrong. I was sure of it. Then the next day, we found out that Doo Doo had been shot and killed on Half Street. It was the dude he called Blast. He's the one who killed him. He killed Doo Doo. Y'all can pick him up and question him about that. I'ma stand on everything I just said."

Joshua Clark was a slightly built man. Brown skinned with long hair and an assuming personality. But he didn't strike me as a tough guy. Grown men with affinities for young girls never were. "Your name is Joshua Clark, no relation to Bryan and Brion Clark, do you have a nickname?"

"Yeah. My nickname is Blood."

"Blood? Are you a Blood gang member? Or did you nickname come from the fact that you rape little girls and get blood on your dick?" Tabitha Kearney asked suddenly.

The look on Joshua Clark's face was one of annoyance and anger. "My uncle nicknamed me that when I was young. He never told me why."

"Well," I said, "Mr. Clark, we can't pick up Blast because he's dead. He was killed as he left Crud's memorial at Stewart's funeral home. But I am interested in two other names you've mentioned. Sean Branch and Quran. What else do you know about Sean Branch and Quran Bashir?"

"Quran Bashir?"

"Yes. The man with Sean that Doo Doo told you killed Whistle, his name is Quran. Full name Quran Bashir. Ever heard of him?"

"Naw. Haven't heard of him. But Sean Branch, I have."

"And what have you heard about Sean Branch?" I asked.

"Just that he's a notorious killer and that he came home after almost 20 years months ago. Dudes in the streets fear him. Him killing Crud and cutting off his head has made him a folk hero in the streets. They say that all he kills is rats and dudes who've crossed him."

I glanced at Tabitha Kearney. "Thank you for introducing me to Blood here. You have my permission to have him moved to a facility out of town to ensure his safety. Try the Alexandria Detention center to keep him close. I might need to talk to him again soon."

***

"It's all hearsay. All the way around the board, Greg." Ari Weinstein emphatically stated.

Ian McNeely stood up and stretched. "Joshua Clark tells a good tale, but that's all it is. A good tale. A good hearsay tale like Ari says. There's no way around it.the Sixth Amendment and the confrontation clause will kill all your good effort. We just learned that a few months ago in the Battle case. And in the Gray case. And in the Darren Williams case and in the Holloway..."

"Okay, Ian. enough with the cases - you've made your point." I scolded. "We have to be able to use this info for something."

"Something like what? The whole story gets tossed before prelims. You can go to a judge and tell that story. You might can find one who's sympathetic to the uptick in homicides and you feed him or her the 'We need to get Sean Branch off the streets to avoid further bloodshed' spiel. Maybe somebody — some judge will go for it. But the fact that we have zero physical evidence to support charges for Sean Branch or Quran Bashir is a glaring deficit."

"Has anyone ever attempted to do a search on any residence associated with Quran Bashir?" Ari Weinstein queried.

"A search?" I repeated. "With what probable cause? We just mention the Sixth Amendment. Do you suggest a way to circumvent the 4th Amendment's assurance against unlawful searches and seizures?"

"Quran Bashir has been mentioned in numerous crimes in the District..."

"And in the state of Maryland, Ari, but that's not probable cause." Ian McNeely spoke next. "Do we even know where Bashir lives? And what about Sean Branch? Do we have addresses for either one of them?"

"Answer your own question for me Ian. find out. Quran Bashir is from Southeast. Ward eight, I believe. Get with someone at 7th District and see if there's any known address for Bashir. Him or his brother Jihad. Ari, you get with your contacts and see if we can get addresses for Sean Branch and Quran Bashir. Once we have those we can further discuss search warrants. Go!"

***

"Bob, I'm glad that you could make it."

"Actually, Greg, I was gonna come and see you anyway. You just saved me a call. I've been getting a lot of information since we last talked and slowly but surely it's all coming together. I need to hear recordings again, though."

"No problem, Bob. Now or later?" I asked Bob Mathis.

"I guess now would be good." He replied.

I cued the computer and let the recordings from Jihad Bashir's cell play.

Twenty minutes later, Bob Marthis had heard enough.

"I'm still convinced that Sean Branch is behind a lot of these murders." Bob proclaimed.

"As do I. I've been saying that since Maurice Payne was killed, then Raquel Dunn and Kenneth Sparrow..."

"Kenneth Sparrow's head was cut off, right?"

I nodded.

"And taken? So far it's never been found, correct?"

"That would be correct."

"Okay. Byron 'Crud' Clark's head was severed from his body, too..."

"It's funny that you mention that. I have something that I want you to hear. Earlier today, one of my assistants brought a man here and I met him. This man had a very interesting story to tell. I recorded that conversation. I want you to listen to it." I extracted the mini recorder from my desk. After setting the volume on 'high' I pushed play.

The full length of the recording was thirty three minutes. Bob Mathis listened to the recording in its entirety. "Whoa! The Gods are smiling down on us. Mildred Best's head was severed from her body and if Sean Branch is the person committing these beheadings, he killed Moe Best's family as well..."

"Any idea why?" I asked.

"Most of the murders we suspect Sean of is retaliatory — well, revenge about past issues. Kenny Sparrow, Reese Payne, Raquel Dunn, Leon Clea, The Kay brothers, etcetera, etcetera. If it's true that he killed Crud, that one would be either for money or a favor for a friend. Namely one of the guys on that case that Crud snitched on. Moe Best's murder would be because word on the street was that Moe Best was a rat and had made past statements on Sean. Trinaboo would be collateral damage. The next significant event would be Sean's daughter getting killed. Most of the murders after that was because Sean Branch is grieving for his daughter and determined to kill anyone who he thinks may have killed her. For instance — Trinaboo's son, Mike, maybe a few others. Sean knows that Moe Best had a big family. He probably killed who he could find now and the other Best boys Kenny and Jeremiah are on his hit list. If the person responsible for all the recent killings is Sean Branch, I hate to mention this but he has access to silencers and hand grenades."

"Silencers and hand grenades? Are you serious?"

"Deathly serious. And we may know where he got them from. Which puts at least six more murders under his belt loop."

"And where would that be?"

"One of the detectives on my unit has been lead investigator on a case where six people were killed in an apartment in a building on Hayes Street in Northeast..."

"I'm familiar with that." I told Bob.

"Well, I found out today that one of the men found in that apartment was Jacob 'Jakey' Gibson and he was under investigation by the ATF for buying and selling military grade weapons. So, I'm assuming that — wait, before I get too ahead of myself. Here's what I found out after I learned about Gibson. I did a check with the Federal Bureau of Prisons and I learned two things — one of which your informant just spoke on. While in the federal system, Sean Branch spent several years incarcerated with Jakey Gibson and a man recently killed on Half Street named..."

"James Yarborough."

Bob nodded. "I cross referenced all of the male names of the recently dead and got a hit on those two names. So, like I was saying earlier, I think Sean hooked up with Gibson in that apartment to buy guns. For some reason Sean ended up killing him and everybody else in that apartment that night. Five people became loose ends that Sean couldn't leave alive. A witness reported seeing a lone man dressed in all black leaving the building with duffle bags and loading them into a vehicle. Now, here's where my detective badge shines bright. Sean Branch somehow knew that Doo Doo — James Yarborough, his friend from prison — knew Byron 'Crud' Clark. Just like your informant says, Sean pays Doo Doo to set Crud up. You know what happened next. But here's what I think happened next. Crud's brother, Brion..."

"Nick named Blast..."

"Right. Blast learns about his brother's death and he wants revenge. Somehow, he gets pointed in Doo Doo's direction. Blast takes Doo Doo to Half Street which is under construction and deserted in the evening. Blast questions Doo Doo then kills him. I'm not exactly sure how, but the two men murdered on Orleans Place is connected to all of this. Maybe Blast killed Miguel Harris that day..."

"Miguel Harris?"

"Yep. He was a known associate of Artinis 'Whistle' Winston, Byron Clark and Doo Doo. Moving right along, somebody ambushes Blast after leaving his brother's memorial at Stewart's. I'm thinking it could've been Sean. Why? I think Doo Doo Yarborough told Blast that Sean Branch killed his brother. I then believe that Blast somehow let it be known that he wanted to kill Sean Branch. Somehow — and I know that these are a lot of somehow — Sean Branch got the message. He goes to Stewart's and kills Blast. Now, here's the plot twist. Brion 'Blast' Clark has a girlfriend. That girlfriend's name is Renaissance Tyler. Do you remember the name Von Tyler?"

"Von Tyler? Of course, I do. Prolific killer in the eighties and nineties. No one was more dangerous than Von Tyler except maybe Ameen Bashir."

"Well, Renaissance is his daughter. And get this, she was at the scene of theOrleans Place murders. She drove Blast there to talk to Miguel Harris and guess what?"

"What?" I asked, curiosity piqued.

"She went there in a red Infiniti truck. Witness saw — identified her as the driver of the vehicle that Brion Clark

IF YOU CROSS ME ONCE 5 | ANTHONY FIELDS

left in. minutes later, a female walked down the block and opened fire on Miguel Harris and two other men. One later died and the other survived."

"So, you think that Renaissance Tyler was inside the red Infiniti truck that Joshua Clark saw pull out behind Blast's silver Lexus the day he picked up Doo Doo from Langston Lane?"

Bob Mathis nodded. "So, that puts her on the scene at Doo Doo's murder. And here's another 'somehow' for you. Somehow, she's stoked Sean Branch's ire because days ago, someone went to Renaissance's mother's house in Ivy City and blew the house up, then killed a teenager named Damien Tyler as he ran out of the burning house. ATF forensic tech's said the blast was created by a hand grenade..."

"Sean Branch."

"Yep. Hours before that, a lone man, dressed in all black went to 832 Southern Avenue and killed a woman on the front porch."

"832 Southern Avenue? That's the address listed in our files for Crud and his brother Blast. Someone killed their sister Bionca?"

"We thought so, but no. Bionca Clark may have been the intended target but she wasn't the victim. The victim was identified as thirty year old Celine James. I definitely believe that all of these *lone* gunmen is one man. Sean Branch. What do you think?"

My sunken mood suddenly brightened. "I think we have enough circumstantial evidence to convince a judge to issue an arrest warrant for Mr. Branch. I need to make some calls, Bob. Did you get what you came here for? The recordings, I mean?"

"I think so. I was looking for clarity and I think between the jail recordings and Joshua Clark, I found what I needed."

"Good. You can show yourself out. I'll be in touch."

"Will do. And with a little luck, we'll catch Sean with one of the heads he's kept for souvenirs."

"Let's keep our fingers crossed."

"And a couple of toes, too."

Chapter 22
Tomasina

It was count time at CTF. Me and my fellow officer Rory Gavin walked both tiers in the unit and counted. "You got 58, Ro?" I asked.

"58 is the right count, Tom. I'ma call it into control."

In the office, I pulled out my cell phone and saw several missed calls. Two of them were from Quran. Smiling to myself, I promised to call him later. Just as I was about to put my phone back in my jacket pocket,it vibrated. The caller was my good girlfriend Jackie Casey. I wasn't supposed to be on my phone while on the job, but I said, 'fuck it' to myself and answered the call. "Jack, what's up?"

"Where you at, Tom?" Jackie asked.

"I'm at work, bitch. Why?"

"You still going to fast Eddies with me tonight? Backyard be turnt up on Wednesday nights. I'm tryna dance, prance and fake some romance. Donnie's goofy ass done got locked up out Maryland, so I'm tryna find a new dick to sit on. Preferably one with length, girth and curve. And a few dollars in the pockets of its owner wouldn't hurt."

I laughed at Jackie. "And you think you gon find all that at Fast Eddies?"

"Why not? Them niggas with that cash love to party with Backyard still. And you know that I'ma bad bitch. A bad bitch who's a dick magnet. A big dick magnet."

"Bitch, don't you mean a big disease magnet? What was it last time? Chlamydia or Trichamonis?"

"Fuck you, Tom. you always joning and shit."

"Joning? Jack, I'm dead serious. You better slow your ass down before you end up honeymooning in Vegas out here. You are my girl. I love you, but I'm serious. Just because Donnie got locked up don't mean that your Vanessa Williams looking ass gotta get some new dick. That new dick be coming with issues. Baby mamas, other side bitches, drama — and that honeymoon in Vegas."

"Tom, chill out with all that shit. Don't you know that words got power. Don't speak no shit like that into the universe."

"I feel you, but let me ask you this before I go. What would your crazy ass do if you did catch that shit?"

"Fuck you think I'ma do? Give that shit right back to other niggas. Shit — I wouldn't be the only muthafuckin dummy out here sick. Niggas would get this pussy gift wrapped and handed to 'em. It's the gift that keeps on giving."

I cracked up laughing. "That's exactly what I thought you'd say. You crazy as shit, but I love you, though. Yeah, I'm with you, but I'ma have to meet you there. I get off at twelve. I'ma have to go home, shower and change clothes, then I'm there. I'ma call you when I leave here."

"Aight, Tom. Love you, bitch."

"Love you more. Bye."

***

Central Treatment facility
1901 E Street SE
12:05 a.m.

When I arrived at my car, there was someone leaning next to it. I reached into my purse to extract my mace. As I approached closer, the person turned around. Quran smiled a cocksure smile.

"Did I scare you?"

"Who me? Never that. I'm from Southeast. Southeast don't breed no scared bitches. What are you doing here? Leaning on my car at midnight. In the cold." Quran pulled his Moncler skull cap lower on his head. The navy blue skullie matched the navy blue metallic Moncler ski coat he wore. Jeans and all gray New Balance rounded out his outfit. "I been calling you and you ain't been answering. I know that you got off work at twelve, so here I am."

My Channel peacoat was buttoned all the way up so that the collar on my coat covered my neck and chin. I wasn't wearing a hat and my ears were starting to get cold. "Let's talk in the car, I'm freezing out here."

Once in the car, Quran said, "I don't know what the fuck is going on with me, but I been missing you, Tom. That's number one. Number two, I need you to hit lil bruh and Dave off again..."

My cell phone vibrated. It was Jackie. "Wait, let me get this." I answered the call. "What, Jackie? I just got off."

"Aight, bitch. Hurry your ass up home and wash that poopoo then get your ass up here. I'm already inside."

"Damn, you was pressed like shit. I'll be there shortly."

"Aight. Bye."

I put the cell phone in the center console. "Now, where were we?"

"Where are you going when I leave?"

"Damn, nigga." I said and smiled. "First you in here getting all mushy talking about you miss a bitch and now you're questioning me? Aw-w-w, is this pussy making you possessive?"

Quran laughed. "I don't know about all that. It's torch, though."

"Is that right? It's just torch and nothing else?" I asked salaciously.

"Torch is top of the line. It don't get no better..."

"Let's see." I said and kicked off my Nike boots. I removed my peacoat, and tossed it in the backseat. I pulled my uniform shirt out of my pants and undid my belt. Lifting up, I slid out of my pants. Once my pants were off my panties followed. I leaned over and unzipped Quran's jeans, reached inside his pants and pulled his dick free.

Getting up on my knees, I bent over his lap and kissed his dick all over, then licked it like an ice cream cone. After taking it deep into my mouth a few times, I rose up completely. "I'ma bout to fuck your jeans up, Que." Maneuvering onto his lap, I grabbed Quran's erection and placed it at the opening to my center. Then before he could protest or say a word, I slid down his pole. My lips found Quran's lips and my tongue darted out. I licked his lips, kissed his nose, tongued his cheeks and neck. All the while, I rode him. soft moans escaped his mouth and I caught those too. Kissed them, licked them, inhaled them. I felt that familiar stirring inside me and knew that my orgasm was going to be epic. I laid my head on Quran's shoulder and grinded myself into a blue funk. One that reminded me of the past. I felt high and euphoric. My impending climax was quickening my heart rate. Then, with a series of moves, it happened. I came in gushes that saturated Quran's jeans. A few minutes later, he exploded, too.

***

"Here," Quran said and handed me a small bag. "These are new phones, sim cards and chargers. The weed is packaged already. One for the both of them." Quran reached into his pocket and pulled out a wad of cash. He passed it to me. "And this is for you."

"For the good time you just had or for getting contraband to your folks." I replied with a smile.

"Both. And to answer your question from earlier, I think that pussy is making me possessive. In a good way, though."

"Boy, stop! I'm supposed to be at Fast Eddie's getting my party on. My friend Jackie gon kill me."

"If she does, I promise you, I'll avenge you." With that said, Quran exited the car and disappeared in the night.

Chapter 23
Quran

Still no word at all from Sean. I didn't know if he was dead or alive. But due to the volume of homicides in the city, I honestly believed that Sean Branch was the main reason for the majority of recent deaths. I thought about our last meeting and how Sean had come totally unglued. It was sad and humiliating to watch. To me, the big homie was a Marvel comics hero. Something like the Incredible Hulk. To see him appear human was uncomfortable for me. The numbers that I had for Sean had in my phone,no longer worked. With my hands laced together and behind my head, I laid on top of the bed in my condo and stared at the ceiling fan. I'd been up for the last twenty hours straight. I'd sexed both Zin and Tomasina and yet, I felt no fatigue. Sleep couldn't find me. Inside the bedroom, it was a little cold because I hadn't turned the heat on, but I was oblivious to it. I was comfortable in street clothes that I still had on. My jeans were stained with Tomasina's cum and my clothes reeked of her scent. I thought about the beautiful woman who gave me Erykah Badu vibes with her swag and humor. There was something about her that drew me to her like bees to honey. The situation with Tom would have to end at some point and when it did, I hoped to have no regrets. The recent text messages were from Halima Ndugu. Bo's aunt had been out of the country for the last month, but wanted to see me when she returned in a few days. Those thoughts brought on thoughts of the other woman in my life. KiKi Swinson. So far, things between me and KiKi hadn't progressed past recent phone calls. Her schedule was always altered and in flux. She had since dropped a new urban novel entitled Pussy Hound and was touring the country promoting it. I missed her strictly because of her nastiness during sex. Thinking of pure nasty acts during sex made me think about the woman that I had killed. Tosheka's voice came to mind then as I listened to her getting fucked by Jihad. Had I been sneakily jealous of the two of them? Was that the real reason that I had pronounced Tosheka guilty of being a potential threat and neutralized it? Those questions threatened to haunt me for the rest of my life. One by one, I kicked off my shoes. They hit the hardwood floor with a thud. I thought about Mike Carter. I thought about what Sean had told me. Was it true that Mike had had an affair with my mother? Had my mother gotten pregnant by him? Was Khitab really Mike Carter's son and not Ameen Bashir's? Had my father ever learned of my mother's betrayal? Did he know that Khitab was not his son? Did Mike Carter really kill my father? All because he thought or knew for sure that my father was having a continuous affair with Patricia Carter?

I thought about the fact that I hadn't talked to Mike Carter in a couple weeks. According to Zin, she'd told her father about us. Why hadn't Mike called to confront me about the secrets I'd kept from him? There's been no contact at all. No contracts given, none taken. Not having names on a list and people to kill was disconcerting to me. I felt a void in my life that sexing several women all day, didn't fill. I needed to find something else to do with my life.

"You should start a business of some kind." A voice in my head said.

"You got the money to do anything that you need to do."

Starting a business was a good idea. Maybe it was passed time to transition from a killer street dude to businessman. There was nothing more than clothes that I loved. Maybe I'd open a clothing shop. A high end urban boutique. I laid in the bed and shook my feet. With several impending murder investigations breathing down my back and hovering like an ever present shadow, it was definitely time for a life change. I closed my eyes and suddenly sleep found me.

Chapter 24

Sean Branch
Curry & Sons Crematorium
White Plains, MD

The road was slick with snowfall slush. I switched the controller to four wheel drive in the stolen Toyota Tundra. In my rearview mirror, I saw the black Honda Accord that followed behind me. In front of my truck was a white cargo van with Curry and Son's emblazoned across both of its sides. At the side entrance to the crematorium, the van came to an abrupt stop. I watched as two attendants worked diligently to offload the gurneys with the bodies on them. A knock on my passenger window caught my attention. I turned back to see the bodies enter the building.

The door opened and a woman climbed into the passenger seat of the Tundra. "Don't like this, Sean. this ain't right." My aunt Carolyn said. "They deserve proper burials. Good Christian burials. My sister would have..."

"Never stepped one foot inside of anybody's church. My mother hasn't been to church in decades. She was against all that organized bullshit. You know how private she was. She's was my mother for forty two years and she never once mentioned that she wanted to buried or viewed..."

"Sean, please listen to me. While you were in jail. Sharon and I talked a lot over the years. She may have been a little disenchanted with the church but she still loves Jesus.

Cremation is a sin, Sean. It's not the right thing to do. Your mother would not have wanted this.

Neither would Shontay. Don't do this to them. Let me put together a double funeral for them. I'll pay..."

I laughed a demonic laugh, then turned to face my mother's youngest sister. "I'm not cremating my mother and daughter because it's cheaper than a traditional funeral and burial. I don't need you to pay for shit. I just needed you to come here and claim the bodies because I couldn't. I could've, but then the police would know where I am. And even though I'm not on the run – yet, they'd love to track me. Why? Because the police in DC know exactly what I'm on. They know that I'm distraught about my daughter's murder and my mother's suicide. And they know that I'm killing people, Aunt Carolyn. They know that. And they're right. I have been killing people non stop since I got home. I have stepped up the number of people I've killed since Shontay was killed and my mother took her own life. The police in DC and Maryland know that I'm not going to stop until I'm dead. Killing my daughter was a mistake. One that a lot of innocent people have paid for and will continue to pay for. My enemies should have left her out of our beef. But they didn't and now family members like you who left DC have to come back and bury entire families. Because of me, my grief and my appetite for revenge. 'Vengeance is mine', sayeth the Lord. Does your bible say that?"

Carolyn nodded. "It says that, but..."

"But what?" I said and laughed. "I'm not the Lord?"

"No, you're not. You gotta let God deal with this, Sean. please stop all the stuff you're doing. All the killing. In my sister's name. In Shontay's name. Stop it. Give it to God. Please..."

I couldn't contain my laughter for some reason. "Vengeance is mine, sayeth the Lord and I'm the Lord. I am God. I hold people's lives in MY hands. I decide if they live or die. I punish or I give MERCY. I love and I hate. I do all the things that the Lord does. So, I'm him. I'ma deal with all of my enemies. And I'm going to continue to kill until I'm one hundred percent sure that I've killed whoever was responsible for killing Shontay. I don't want tombstones and grave markers to remind me of what I lost. So, I'ma cremate my mother and spread her ashes out in a flower bed somewhere. Shontay's ashes will stay in an urn and be put to sea. She was an explorer. Loved to travel. In death, she'll still travel. I appreciate you coming here from Cleveland to claim the bodies — as a matter of fact, here," I reached beneath the seat of the Tundra and pulled a stack of money. I handed the stack to my aunt.

"Take this for your troubles."

Carolyn Reynolds looked at the money as if it was a poisonous spider. "No, thank you, nephew. Keep your money and get it to whoever you get to bury you." my aunt exited the truck and walked back to the Honda.

I smiled to myself as I watched the Honda come to life in my mirror. Seconds later, it was headed back down the road we'd just traveled. Laughing, I got out of the truck and walked up to the crematorium. Inside the establishment, I found someone who led me to the bodies of my loved ones. Both bodies were inside of a body bag. A paper taped to the foot of the gurneys told who was who. Although the morgue's people do all they can to put people's brains back in their heads and beautify a corpse, I had no interest in seeing the destruction that bullets had caused to my mother and daughter. I stood close to the bag that held my daughter. Before I could say a word, my cell phone vibrated with an incoming text. I pulled the phone out of my pocket and looked at the text, then I put it back.

"Babygirl, I'm sorry for what happened to you. I was selfish and dumb. I never imagined that someone would hurt you to hurt me. I was too arrogant, too cocky. I never dreamed that I'd have to see you in death before you saw me. Please, if you can hear me, please forgive me for what I am.

Forgive me for what I've done. Your death is crushing me, babygirl. When you died, I died, too. I'm living, but I'm dead inside. But you can rest assured that I will not stop breathing until I have found out who did this to you and kill them all. Family members included. I promise you that. Rest in peace, babygirl. Wherever you are. If paradise and hell is real, we'll never see each other again." I laughed. "But we both know, you're going to paradise and I'm headed for the depths of the hellfire. But in any event, it was a pleasure loving you, holding you and experiencing life with you. I'm just sorry we couldn't have done it longer... Goodbye, baby. I will always and forever love you. In life and death." I leaned down and kissed the bag where Shontay's face was. Then I left the building.

***

"Slim, I don't think they had nothing to do with Shontay." Darrin 'Dee' Jones said as he sat in the Tundra. "Jew Bey wouldn't not talk about it and Kenny stay so fuckin' drunk, he would've said something, too. The streets talk, but, slim they ain't saying a word about who did that to babygirl. Bullshit ain't nothing. But if you still wanna hit them, I'm with it. Jew Bey is in Passion's house right now. He fuckin' with Passion's sister, Treyona."

"He's in there right now?" I asked.

Dee nodded. "Yeah. He drives that Acura right there." Dee pointed to a burgundy Acura hybrid SUV. "He's been in there since I first texted you."

"You said all this shit about the streets talkin' and what not. What has the streets been saying about who killed Moe Best?"

"You can hear all types of stories about that. Niggas is saying that somebody that Trinaboo set up or scammed did that shit. Depends on who's telling the story. Everybody knows that Moe been tellin' on niggas for years to stay out of jail, niggas is sayin' that he got his about that and Trinaboo was just a casualty of war. Since everybody around the way knows that he tried to bury you on them cold case bodies, you already know that your name has come up alot. Depending on the day, you might hear anything."

"What are the streets saying about their — about the Best family getting crushed at home like that?"

"Again, you already know that your name has been mentioned. Alot. but there's all kinds of stories out there about that, too. Too many to discuss. Niggas is saying that you are on a nut about Shontay. Killing any and everybody..."

Smiling, I turned to face Dee. "And what do you say, Dee?"

Dee looked into my eyes and saw the emptiness in them. His face registered fear. "I don't say shit, big homie. I keep my mouth shut and my thoughts on myself and me chasing this bag. That's all."

"That's good, slim. Real good." I pulled out some money and passed it to Dee. "I appreciate your help, bruh, but I need another favor."

"What's up? What you need?" Dee asked.

"I need you to go and knock on Passion's door and get Jew Bey outside for me. Just get him out front. In front of the building, then you can leave. Tell him that somebody is fuckin with his car or something. Just get him outside and I'ma do the rest."

Dee pocketed the money I gave him. "Bet. I'm on it. In a minute."

It was day time in the city, cold as hell as snowing. There weren't a lot of people outside at all. Montana Avenue at the top near Rhode Island Avenue only had apartments on one side of the street and that benefited me. I climbed out of the Tundra's driver's seat and walked quickly across the street to the side of the building that Dee had disappeared into. I pulled the ARP And waited. Minutes later, I heard voices. I peered around the corner and saw Dee talking to Moe Best's brother Jew Bey. I smiled. With the alacrity of a cat, I rounded the corner and caught both men off guard. By the time either one knew what was happening, I was letting the ARP go. Both men fell to the ground. I ended their lives, quickly, then calmly walked away.

Chapter 25

Zin
Superior Court
501 Indiana Ave. NW

"Mr. McNeely, what is the government's position in this case?" Judge Warren Berger asked.

"Your honor, we have extended a couple different plea offers to the defendant and they have all been rejected. The government is ready to proceed to trial."

"Ms. Carter, is the defendant prepared to go to trial in this matter?"

"We are, your honor, but in light of some recent events that have occurred with my client, Mr. Battle is prepared to accept the government's last plea offer."

Judge Berger looked over papers in front of him. "Mr. McNeely, is the plea offer still on the table?"

"It is, your honor." Ian McNeely said.

"I am reading a plea offer in front of me that says in effect that the defendant can plead to one count of carrying a pistol without a license and the counts of unregistered firearm and unregistered ammunition will be dismissed. Is that correct?"

"Correct, your honor."

"And the government agrees to cap the sentence at thirty six months.?"

"Correct, your honor." Ian McNeely said again.

"And the government is aware that thirty six months is the maximum sentence allowed under the statute for CPWL?"

"We are, your honor."

"So, you're basically asking for the maximum sentence allowed?"

"That's correct, your honor."

"Ms. Carter, this case has been going on for some time now. Is your client prepared to accept the government's plea offer today?"

I took a moment to lean in and ask David about accepting the plea.

"Yeah." David answered. "I wanna get this shit over with."

"Your honor, I have conferred with my client and Mr. Battle has informed me that he would like to accept the government plea offer today."

"Splendid. And would your client also agree to be sentenced today, Ms. Carter?"

Before I could even ask hm, David said, "Tell him, yeah."

"Your honor, my client agrees to be sentenced today as well."

"Mr. McNeely, is the government in opposition to anything I just said?"

"Uh — your honor, I have not conferred with my office, but since a pre sentencing report has already been prepared in this case, I see no reason to oppose the accepting of the plea and the defendant being sentenced today."

"That's great, Mr. McNeely. Would the defendant please stand..."

***

In the holding cage
Behind the courtroom...

"The judge did you a favor." I told David. "He knew that the government was on bullshit by asking for the full thirty six months. Had you went to trial, that was the most you could get sentenced to. So, he sentenced you to twenty four months and three years of supervised release. With time served. You've been in jail for twenty two months. That leaves you with two months to do. But I'm sure that you will be charged with the assault on Warren Stevenson before then. That new charge will hold you at the jail until its resolution. We're halfway to the finish line, David. You did right by getting all of this out of the way now. As soon as I find out any new news, I'll come to CTF to see you. Any questions?"

"Naw, Ms. Carter. I'm good. Just give my man my love and respect." David replied.

"I will. Take care, David. And be cool. No new charges."

David Battle smiled. "I promise. No new charges. Thanks for everything."

"Aight, David. Bye."

***

The weather wasn't that bad, but for the life of me I couldn't figure out why Delores had insisted that we visit Harmony Cemetery today. The wind chill factor had fallen and the snow that fell earlier in the day hadn't accumulated. The ground was still wet and slushy. I arrived at Harmony Cemetery a little after 5pm. Since the cemetery was literally deserted, I spotted Delores' car as soon as I turned into Harmony's gates. I pulled alongside of Delores's Chrysler 300. I removed my heels and put on boots.

Delores Samuels was wrapped up in a heavy coat with a scarf around her neck. Her ever present hijab covered her head. Nothing covered her ears. Delores boots looked stylish. Too stylish for the elements of the day. As I got near Delores, she moved close and embraced me.

"Zin, it's great to see you again, baby. How are you?"

"I'm good, Auntie Delores. Just wondering why you insisted on us coming here today."

Delores smiled. "We've been planning this little outing for weeks and never got it done. Today is as good a day as any. Besides, today is a special day. Come on, let me show you." Before walking away, Delores reached into her car and removed two things. A small broom and a bouquet of roses. Delores handed me the roses. "Here. hold these and follow me. But watch your step. We have a small hill to climb."

Our trek ended after about ten minutes. Delores stopped suddenly and used the broom to clear a brass plate in the ground.

"Your grandmother's grave doesn't have a tombstone. In 1978, there was no money for one. But this is where she's buried."

I stood beside Delores and looked down. The brass plate was about the size of a TV dinner box. But as clear as day, I could read what was engraved on the plate.

PEARL ANN MITCHELL
3-23-42   7-10-78
SUNRISE   SUNSET

"Today is her birthday." I said to myself.

"It is." Delores replied. "Your grandmother would be seventy two years old today, Zin. Had she lived to see it."

"She died at thirty six years old."

"Broken hearts don't care how old you are." Delores pulled a single rose from the bouquet in my hand. "She was a wonderful woman, Zin."

"I wish I could have met her."

"Insha'Allah, baby. One day, you will."

Delores placed the single rose on top of the brass plate. She kissed her fingers, then knelt down and touched the plate. "Rest in Peace, Ms. Pearl." Delores stood and grabbed my hand. "Come on. The next one's not too far from here."

The next grave that we went to did have a tombstone.

"Your uncle Paul Jr. died the same year your mother was born. He was only ten years old."

"But how does he have a tombstone..."

"The money for Paul Jr's funeral and tombstone came from Mississippi. Where exactly, I don't know. But it did. My mother told me that. Your uncle Preston is buried just up that hill. Right next to your aunt Pamela Rose."

At each grave site, we left a single rose. My aunt Pam had no tombstone but my uncle Preston did.

"I know you're asking yourself why Preston has a tombstone and your aunt Pam doesn't. The answer is that your grandmother could only afford Pam's funeral and burial. She couldn't afford a tombstone. And unfortunately, nobody from Mississippi sent money for it. Preston has a tombstone because the city paid for it since he was a ward of the city's only mental institution, the powers that be thought it best to pick up the tab for everything involving your uncle." Delores stopped walking once we reached another gravesite. The tombstone was larger than all the others in the area. I read the name on the stone.

Dontay Samuels
5-11-79   1-17-95

There was an *ayat* from the Holy Quran engraved into the tombstone.

He is Allah. There is no God but he. Neither slumber nor sleep over takes him. To him belongs all that's in the heavens and the Earth. Who is there that can intercedeth in his presence without his permission? He knows what will happen to them in this life and in the Hereafter. And they encompass aught of his knowledge, except as he willeth. His throne extends over the heavens and the earth and he feels no fatigue in guarding and preserving them. He is the most high. The supreme in glory.

"We had his Janazah at Masjid Muhammad. Then he was brought here and buried in accordance to the Quran and Sunnah. I had often heard about what Dontay had become in

IF YOU CROSS ME ONCE 5 | ANTHONY FIELDS

the streets. What he did alone and with Quran Bashir. I'd heard all the rumors of all the people Dontay and Quran had killed at your fathers behest. And I knew that a lot of what I had heard was true. I saw the blood that stained my son's clothes on occasion. I saw the blood that soiled his shoes. I knew that he'd become a monster in people's eyes. But to me, he was my son, my baby. My only child. My heart. I loved that boy so much. Still do."

I looked at Delores and saw that her face was now stained with tears. I embraced her and held her in my arms.

Chapter 26
David Battle
Central Treatment facility
Medical Unit
10:03 p.m.

"C'mon, Battle, we don't have a lot of time." Tomasina told me.

I followed her into the medical examination room and shut the door behind me. I wondered if she was just dropping off the pack or about to give me some. My question was answered quickly. Tomasina reached into her pants after unbuckling her belt. She squatted a little and pulled her hand out of her panties.

"Here," Tomasina said and passed me a phallus shaped condom filled with compressed weed. "He didn't send no cigarettes..."

"I don't smoke them joints anyway." I mentioned.

Next, Tomasina pulled a small baggie out of her panties. Inside I could make out a cell phone. "I couldn't bring the charger right now, I got a hot ass supervisor manning the metal detector where we come in at. So, I'ma have to get that to you tomorrow. The phone is fully charged, though. So you can call Quran whenever. His new number is already in the phone."

With a freaky look on my face, while Tomasina was watching, I smelled the condom filled with weed. And then the phone. Tomasina smiled. "My pussy don't stink, boy."

"Never said it did. I just needed a whiff."

"For what?"

"For later on, when I 'm in my bunk with my dick out, stroking it."

"Do you beat your dick a lot?"

"Enough to be charged with domestic violence."

Tomasina laughed, "You are almost as crazy as me." But then she turned her back and pulled her pants down. Her panties went next. "Almost." Tomasina looked back over her shoulder as she spread her ass cheeks. She reached out and grabbed something that came out of her ass.

I stood transfixed to my spot as I watched Tomasina pull the phallus shaped package out her ass completely.

She put the package on the counter by the sink and turned to look over her shoulder. "Don't just stand there, nigga. My ass feels empty. Put your dick in it and fill it up for me."

Shaking my head, I moved quickly behind Tomasina. I couldn't believe my good fortune as I pulled my dick out and slowly slid it deep into her ass.

***

"Tomorrow, I'ma bring Jihad's phone and both chargers. And as always, Quran sends his love." Tomasina said as we exited the exam room. "Go ahead back to your cell. Put that shit up somewhere and be careful with it. Don't get caught..."

"I know the drill. Trust me." I replied

"You I trust, it's these geeking ass, hating ass male COs I don't trust."

True dat. I got you, though. And thank you for everything."

"Thank Quran. I do it for him."

***

In the cell, I unwrapped the phone and flushed the baggie that it came in. I turned the phone in my hand. It was a small LG modeled smartphone. Powering it on, I checked the contacts and sure enough there was a number already in it. I tapped on the number and the phone connected the call.

The other end rang three times before being answered. "Assalamu Alaikum."

"Walaikum assalam." I said, returning the Arabic greeting. "What's up, slim? You good?"

"As can be. Glad to be back on line with you. You got everything I sent?" Quran asked.

"And then some, bruh. And then some. You the best slim. Gotta take my hat off to you. Always find a way to make shit happen."

"That's what I do. You know how I get down. I heard about the sentencing. That's good news. Now we work on that goofy ass assault charge."

"Slim, I feel retarded as shit for even catching that anything ass joint. But it is what it is. I own it. I'm standing on it ten toes down like a soldier should. I really appreciated the response that was sent. Real talk."

"Sayless, homie. Sayless. Real niggas do real things."

"Always, slim. As they should. I would've done the same."

"What's understood already doesn't need to be explained. Enjoy yourself with that loud. Best in the country. I got it from the hot bitch KD from the Cordas. Before she died. Feel me?"

"Absolutely. Again, I respect you to the fullest, slim. Can't wait to see you and really embrace your spirit."

"Patience is a virtue. You will soon. You and Jay. did he get his jack, yet?"

"Naw. baby girl said tomorrow. But I got his loud. He'll get it in the a.m."

"Aight, slim, I'm out. Holla if you need anything." Quran said.

"Aight, bruh. Love you, slim." I disconnected the call and dialed Tiera's number. I reached into my boxer briefs and rubbed my dick, then smelled my hand. "Damn, even that bitch ass smells good."

Chapter 27
Tomasina

"Hey, Samuels." The officer whose post was at the staff entrance to CTF called out.

"Hey, Thomas. How are you?" I replied as I approached the metal detector on the way out the door. "Still mad about them bum ass Redskins?"

"Talk all you want. Samuels, but y'all wasn't saying all that bum shit when we ran through the whole NFL in 2012. If RG111 didn't get hurt in that playoff game against Seattle..."

"If I woulda, coulda, shoulda. That shit was two years ago, bro. How long does it take for a quarterback to come back from a messed up leg? RG111 ain't done shit since the NFL caught up to that fake ass RPO bullshit he brought from Baylor. Just face it, booboo, y'all some shit now and y'all will always be some shit..."

"Whatever. Y'all Cowboys fans always talk shit but y'all just as bad as us. Cold blooded shit cakes. Admit it. We ain't won a Super Bowl since 1992, y'all ain't done it since, what? 1995?"

"We got five Super Bowl rings, though. How many y'all got?"

"We got three. Half of the teams in the league ain't got three Super Bowls under their belts. We gon' be aight. Watch."

I walked through the metal detector. "Whatever. I need to run to the car for a minute, Thomas. I'll be right back."

"Aight. Take your time. No worries."

***

I noticed the burgundy Hyundai Sonata parked next to my car as soon as I approached. Images of Quran outside my car the night before came to mind. I smiled at the images of what happened in the car moments later. The driver's side door of the Hyuandi opened and a woman stepped out. The lights that illuminate the parking lot seemed to dance off of the colors in her hijab. "Why are you here?"

Delores Samuels smirked. "You know why, I'm here, Tom. don't fuckin' play with me. If you'd answer my calls, I wouldn't have to show up at your job and wait for you to come outside."

"Been working double shifts everyday for about the last month or so."

"I get that, but you can still return my calls, Tom."

"Why should I do that, Dee, when I already know what you want? I already know what questions you wanna ask."

"Is that right? And what questions do I wanna ask?"

"Have you gotten close to Quran? Does he have a clue who you really are? And when are you gonna complete the plan? How's that for clairvoyance?"

Delores smiled. "Never knew you were psychic, Tomasina. But since you already know what questions I wanna ask, why don't you do me a favor and answer them."

"I don't like to be pressured, Dee."

"Nobody's pressuring you, Tom. you came up with the plan to avenge Dontay's death after all these years and I loved the plan. This was your idea. An idea that I absolutely need to see manifest. That's why I'm here. But still, no pressure."

I laughed to myself. "No pressure, huh? Listen, Mrs. Delores, I am a woman of my word. Always have been, always will be..."

"The questions, Tomasina. Answer the questions."

"Have I gotten close to Quran Bashir? Yes. Our friendship has evolved into a more deeper one..."

"You're fucking him?" Delores blurted out.

"I'm doing whatever I need to do to disarm him and build his trust. I have to do that before I can even think about killing him. So, if you must know, I fuck him, suck his dick, whatever it takes. You should know that better than anyone."

"What the fuck is that supposed to mean?"

"You know what the fuck it means. How did you get my father from my mother?"

Delores Samuels facial expression changed to fury. "You know what? If we didn't have a common goal — a common enemy, I would whip your ass out here."

"You could try, Dee, but you wouldn't succeed. I'm tryna respect my elders and you making it hard for me. Talking that slick shit. I can't stay out here all day, so let me finish this by saying, no, Quran does not know who I really am. How could he? All he knew was you, Dontay and my father. He never knew that Donnie Samuels had other children by other women. And since I was so young, Dontay probably never talked to Quran about me. So, he has no clue that I'm Dontay's sister. And lastly, I'm going to do exactly what I told you I would. I am going to kill Quran Bashir. And just to give his death an exclamation point, I'm going to kill his brother Jihad, too. When? Soon. Very soon. Does that answer your questions?"

Delores Samuels capitulated. "I guess it does."

"Good. now, if you'll excuse me, I have things to do." I said. And got into my car. As I fished out the cell phone for Jihad Bashir, I could hear Delores' car come to life. I glanced around and saw the tail lights on her car as she drove away. "That bitch has got some nerve." I muttered to myself.

"Showing up at my job questioning me about my intentions. Dontay was her son and her scary ass ain't did shit to avenge his death. All these fuckin' years, her ex crack head ass ain't done shit. And now that I confide in her about getting back at the man who killed my brother, her ass is suddenly super involved. Bitch, please. Kill yourself. Talking about you gon whip my ass. Where was all that energy years ago when you saw Quran in the hood everyday and never said shit. Never did shit?" I got everything that I needed out of the car. Still steaming from the conversation with my father's wife, I did what needed to be done. I put the cell phone in plastic and wrapped it tight. Then I squatted a little and put the package inside my panties. With a little push it disappeared inside my wet pussy.

***

Back inside the jail, I walked around the metal detector after giving Jeffrey Thomas a wink. He didn't say a word. I thought about the fact that I had told David that I'd bring Jihad's phone in the next day. "But why put off for tomorrow what you can do today?" I said to myself earlier and decided to give Jihad Bashir his just due. In every way possible. It took me five minutes to reach the Medical Unit. After I was buzzed in, I walked straight into the office.

"Back so soon." Carmen Rodriguez, the CO on duty asked.

"Yeah, boo. Do me a favor and pop out Jihad Bashir."

"Anything for you, Tom. Anything for you."

Chapter 28
Quran

"Quran, baby, it's late as shit and I gotta get up early." Zin said and yawned. "I love you baby, but I need some sleep."

"Damn, and here I thought I was making leeway in tryna get you to let me come over and do some things. Now, you're curving me. I should've just used my key to get in and just took you with no questions asked."

"Well, you should have. But you didn't. Your loss, sir. That's what you get for talking on the phone for thirty minutes. Next time, less talk and more action. And since you mentioned it, do not come here, Quran. I'm serious. I got like four court appearances to make and a visit to three different jails."

"Three different jails?"

"Yes. DC jail, CTF and I gotta go to Alexandria Detention Center. The US Marshal separated one of my clients from his co-defendant and I need to find out why. From him"

"Everybody they send out there ain't fucked up, but make sure your clients understands that we ain't representing no rats. Real live."

Zin laughed. "We? We ain't repping no rat? Since when did you become a lawyer?"

"I didn't. I'm the judge, jury and executioner."

"Bye, Quran and you need to watch what you say on the phone. Any phone. Mine could be bugged, too. I'm about to go to sleep. I'll talk to you tomorrow, Mr. Executioner."

"Aight. Get some sleep. I love you, Zin."

"Love you, more. Goodnight."

The call ended and I glanced to my right out of the tinted window of the Genesis. The house on Seawood Lane looked exactly as I remembered it when I was last here. I sent a quick text and received an even quicker reply. Smiling, I got out of the car and felt the accumulated snow crunch underfoot. I walked around the car and up the path that led to 11441. As I got close to the front door, it opened. Halima Ndugu appeared in the doorway like an apparition. Her hair was braided in a thick braid that fell down her chest and back. Her ebony skin tone was beautiful as always. I moved closer to Halima and noticed that the robe she wore had opened to reveal her ample breasts, her runway strip of pubic hair and her phat pussy. My eyes traveled down. Her toes were perfectly pedicured with a doll pink tone that matched her fingernails and lip gloss. I walked right up into her arms. I lifted Halima and stepped further into the foyer.

"You have to close the door, Quran." Halima whispered to me.

Letting her down, I backpedaled and shut the door, then locked it. Once that was done I went back to Halima and lifted her again. I threw her over my shoulder and walked into the room where the fireplace was raging. Gently, I let Halima down and laid her on the carpet in front of the fireplace. The fire's warmth enveloped me instantly. I removed my coat, sweatshirt, wife beater, pants, boxer briefs, boots and socks. Removing Halima's robe was next. A diamond ankle bracelet sat at the base of Halima's left leg. I started there. I licked all over her left ankle and moved down to her foot. While rubbing Halima's right foot, I tongue bathed her left foot and toes. Then I moved to the right one. After paying attention to Halima's feet and luxuriating in the fire's warmth and her soft moans, I moved up to Halima's thighs, then to her wet center. Juices flowed from Halima like water from a fountain and I drank it all in. enjoyed the flavor of it all. After I'd quenched my thirst, I was ready to be inside of Halima. "Turn over." I told her. Halima complied with my order, she turned completely over and laid on her stomach. Her ass rose from the small of her back like hills in plain. I kissed both cheeks before laying down on top of her. Grabbing Halima's hair. I moved her braids to give me access to her neck. Her neck smelled of fruit. I bit her neck as I simultaneously entered her. Halima's lips parted and the noises she made turned me on. My mind and body found a rhythm and played Halima's body like an instrument. I grinded deeper and deeper into her. And all Halima could do was call out my name.

"Quran — Quran — Quran!!"

Chapter 29
Greg Gamble

"In the throes of an escalating scandal involving DCs United States Attorney Gregory Gamble, his office has filed suit against two landlords this week for allegedly allowing properties to fall into dangerous disrepair. The lawsuit accuses one landlord of using harassment and poor living conditions to push longtime residents out and the other of ignoring dangerous conditions for more than six years. Officials at the US Attorney's Office said that the lawsuits are part of ongoing efforts to address issues of neglect and displacement in affordable housing properties. In both cases, the District is asking a judge to appoint a third-party, answerable to the courts, to oversee emergency repairs to bring the properties up to code. US Attorney Greg Gamble says that acts being perpetrated by the landlords are criminal and his office is seeking indictments for egregious violations against the properties residents. The two properties involved in the lawsuits are Hawaii-Webster Apartments in Ward 5. The property is an eleven building complex made up of 88 garden style apartments. The second property is King Towers, a rent controlled building in Ward 2 with 129 apartments. More than half of the tenants receive housing assistance from the government..."

"Greg, come to bed." Martin Mayhew said as he silenced the TV with the remote. "Why do you inundate your brain with all that foolishness that the media perpetuates everyday? Is it the investigations that worry you and make you lose sleep?"

"Did you know that on Wednesday, the United States Senate confirmed three DC judicial nominees?" I replied.

"No, I did not, but what does that have to do with anything I just..."

"The DC Superior Court and its DC Court of Appeals were confronting a record 19 total empty seats. Sixteen of which were in Superior Court, a quarter of its entire branch. I could have filled one of those seats, Marty. Everything was fine until this whole Michael Carter thing reared its ugly head. All the things I've done for this city, all the changes I've made to bring about change. To get rid of its most dangerous criminals. I single handedly lowered the homicide rate in the nineties into the two thousands. I sent over two thousand criminals to prison during my tenure at the US Attorney's office. I have a friend at the Judicial Nomination Commission and I was told that I was a lock for a judge ship if I continued to work hard and keep my nose clean. Well, Marty, not only is my nose not clean anymore, it's bleeding. Profusely."

Martin moved around the sofa and stood directly in front of me. He dropped down to his knees and placed his hands on mine. "Greg, everything is going to be alright. No matter what that woman said in court, nobody can ever prove that you paid her to commit those crimes. Your career has been stellar at 555 4th Street and no one can dispute that. It's after midnight, baby. Come to be and let me make you feel better."

"Sounds good, Marty, but I can't sleep. I need to think. I have to prepare myself."

"Prepare yourself for what?"

"I've been summoned to the office of the Attorney General. Tomorrow. I have to prepare myself for whatever is said at that meeting. I'm fighting for my career and I'm not going to lay down."

"The Attorney General is still Paul Danielson, correct?"

I nodded. "Correct."

"Don't you have a file on him, too?" Martin asked.

That's when I allowed myself a brief smile. "Of course I do."

Chapter 30

Ren Tyler
Ren's apartment
1:17 a.m.

"According to the news and the word around town, when Sean Branch's mother found out about her granddaughter getting killed, she ate a gun and offed herself." Bionca said. My head laid in her lap. "That's a two for one. But here's the thing, it's been what? A couple weeks since that happened and still no death notice online or in the Washington Post. I think that Sean is too smart to be tricked by the same trick he pulled on us. Think about it. We made it super easy for him to get to Brion. My stupid ass posted the death notice about Crud in the paper and online. I paid to do that. I told you and I told Brion that Sean Branch was a different type of killer. I knew that he was a throwback killer..."

"Throwback killer? Fuck is that?" I asked.

"A killer who operates on old principles. He has to be about forty two or forty three. So, that makes him a seventies baby. He grew up in a different era. He was raised in what I call the throwback era. The era when DC was on some different shit. Not like it is now. In Sean Branch's era, DC niggas had to deal with outta town niggas in all the hoods. When Sean was coming up, killing was different. Killers were different."

"Like my father. My father was a vicious muthafucka, Bee."

"I heard about him a lot before he died. I was connected to all street niggas, hustlers, gamblers, stickup niggas coming up. I was fascinated by my oldest brother and all the dudes like him. I was a young bitch that hid my fascination with all things street from my family. Crud or my mother never knew it, but I jumped off the porch at a very young age. Starting fucking at eleven years old. Smoking, drinking, holding niggas shit. Hustling a little bit, playing with guns. I was into all of that shit by the time I was thirteen. I been pregnant three times, got three abortions, took a beef for a nigga. I been wifey. I been the side bitch. I even killed two people, Ren. I'm telling you all of this to make you understand that I ain't no square bitch and when I tell you some real shit I mean it. I been in these DC streets all my muthsfuckin' life. I've experienced a lot of shit. Shit that I have never told a soul and probably won't. I know what I know. Feel me?"

"I feel you."

"Good. Sean Branch is throwback because young niggas today are not built like niggas was in the eighties. DC niggas went toe to toe with real street niggas, real killers from New York, Miami, California, Jamaica, Panama, Hispanics, mob niggas — all that shit. They stepped to that shit and won all the wars. That's why the feds is fulla DC niggas that got kicked out of Lortin. Where else on the planet have you ever heard of an entire prison system throwing in the towel because of the viciousness of its prisoners? You haven't. But that's what happened. Lorton, Virginia wanted no more parts of them niggas. Why? Because they were all throwback killers. They lived through one of the roughest periods that the nation's capital has ever seen. DC was the murder capital for like four years in a row. Sean Branch was responsible in part for a lot of the murders that made DC the murder capital. But that's not the only reason I call dudes like Sean a throwback. Think about it, what you heard and what you know about your father. Compare him to the youngins that catch all the bodies of today. You can't can you? Of course not. Why? Because a lot of shit was different then compared to now. Killers today have a lot of help. They got guns that hold more rounds. They got extended clips and shit with switches. They got shit that goes from semi automatic to fully with a touch of a finger. Nowadays, these niggas got guns and rifles from every country in the world. They got hand guns that fire choppa bullets. Niggas didn't have that shit back in the day. They had revolvers and pump shotguns, ten shot Berettas, cheap ass Glocks and anything ass handguns of all sorts. And niggas back then didn't 'spin the bend' and kill everybody but their target. Throwback killers back then just walked up and blew your brains out. They hid in cars, under cars, in trash cans, in pissy hallways. They dressed up in disguises. Wasn't no shooting a hundred shots from across the street. They pulled up, hopped out and crushed shit. Then simply walked away. They caught niggas at school, at work, at church, at home, out eating, whereever. Throwback niggas killed niggas in the barber chair. They walked in restaurants and left your shit on the plate. Throwback niggas killed in hospital rooms. Throwback niggas stopped the ambulance, got into the back and killed their target. I knew exactly what kind of person Sean Branch was — I told Brion about Sean, but he wasn't prepared to hunt him. You wasn't prepared to hunt him. I should have told Brion to stand down. At least until..."

"He wouldn't have listened."

"I know that but I still should have tried to stop him, stop you. Made sure that y'all knew what you were up against. Made sure that y'all knew that it wasn't a good idea to attend Crud's memorial AFTER y'all had tried to ambush Sean. I blame myself for that. I was supposed to have known that Sean would come there. I knew what he was and totally overlooked the throwback shit he would do.

I made it easy for him. And he did exactly what any throwback killer would do. Go to the memorial of the man he killed to find the family. Especially the brother who had shot at him. And I've come to the conclusion that Sean was probably at Stewart's the entire time. Waiting for Brion. And you. The only reason you're still a live Ren is because you going to the bathroom after the service saved your life. Had you never went and taken the pregnancy test, you'd have left Stewart's with Brion. You'd have been right there with him in that parking lot and Sean Branch would have killed you both."

My eyes filled with tears. They fell from my eyes before I could wipe them away.

"I thought about that several times. I came to the same conclusion. And every time I do, I get mad at myself for going in that restroom. I was supposed to have been there by his side. Died right there by his side..."

"Ren, don't say..."

"I gotta say it because it's true. Had I died that day in that parking lot with Blast, we'd be together now. In the afterlife, wherever that may be. And I'd prefer that to this. Living here without Blast ain't living. It ain't."

"It's gonna get easier, Ren. time heals..."

"It's not. It don't. Stop saying that shit because it ain't true, Bionca, it ain't."

The next thing I felt was Bionca's fingers wiping away my tears from my cheeks and eyes. I felt her hand as it moved through my hair. Her hand on my face smells like citrus bath and body soap. I felt Bionca as she leaned down. She whispered to me. "It takes a throwback to trap a throwback. And even though I'm young, I fit the bill. You'll feel a lot better after we've killed Sean Branch. That'll bring you some peace. I promise."

Then Bionca's lips found mine.

IF YOU CROSS ME ONCE 5 | ANTHONY FIELDS

Chapter 31
Det. Bob Mathis

Being a cop in a city like DC comes with its highs and its lows, but I embrace them both. I opened up the small baggie and dumped its contents out onto the kitchen table. Taking out my gold badge from my wallet, I pried the badge loose from its laminate. I used the badge to separate the pile of powder on the table top. Then I flattened the badge on the section closest to me. I pressed down hard to break up all the little rocks of heroin that I saw. Once that was done, I made lines of dope from the pile in front of me. Long lines. I lowered my nose to the beginning of the line and sniffed as much of the line as I could into my nostril. Then I repeated the exercise with the other nostril. Coughing a bit, I felt the heroin start to drain in my nasal passage. The bitterness of it made me frown. I moved to the refrigerator and opened it. I could taste the heroin in my throat as it hit my system like a ton of lumber. Quickly, I removed the orange juice from the fridge and opened it. I took a generous swig straight from the bottle.

"You brought a treat home, I see." A female voice behind me said. Taking another swig of juice from the bottle, I turned to see my live-in girlfriend, Veronica 'Ronnie' Williams standing by the table eyeing the heroin. She was dressed in nothing but cotton panties. "Help yourself." I told Ronnie. "Be careful, though, it's some good shit. Raw."

"Your brother called the house phone. Said you wasn't answering your cell." Ronnie said before making a quill out of paper that was on the table.

"Which one?" I asked. Eddie or Peaches?"

Ronnie used the quill to snort the last of the first line of dope I'd left. Then she snorted some of the second line. She squeezed both nostrils as she threw her head back and sniffed. "Eddie — damn, this is good dope. Instant drain. Burns a little and nasty as shit. Gimme some of that OJ."

I passed the orange juice to Ronnie as she approached. "Eddie don't want shit. Lil Eddie or Corey probably done got into a jam. I'll call him back later today." I could feel the heroin's calming effect on me. I could feel myself about to go into a good nod.

The orange juice jar being sat on the table loudly caught my attention. Ronnie looked at me with a wicked smile on her face. "Uh uh, nigga. You can stop all that 'you in your jam' shit. You been working around the clock for weeks and I ain't said shit. But now I need some dick and I ain't tryna wait. I been patient as hell. I'm tired of being patient. Without the dope, you are an animal in bed, but with it in you, you're a beast. That's what I need right now. C'mon."

Before I could protest, my hand was pulled and I ended up in the living room of my house.

"C'mon, Rob, we ain't even gotta go upstairs. Ain't nobody here but us. We gon fuck right here."

Ronnie was the only person that called me Rob instead of Bob, but I liked it. She made it sound sexy. I struggled to keep my eyes open as Ronnie wiggled out of her panties. She climbed up onto the couch on all fours, her face buried in the cushions.

I undressed quickly. Once I was naked, I walked up behind Ronnie and entered her. Her pussy was soaking wet. "Your pussy wet as shit."

"You just made it that way. Stop talking and fuck me!"

I grabbed Ronnie by the waist and looked at her ample ass. Licking my thumb, I slid it into her tight ass.

"Don't do — that — Rob — o-o w-w-w!"

Pushing my thumb even further, I moved it in and out until I was in Ronnie's ass to the knuckle. My dick matched the piston action. I looked down and saw the thick, creamy cum at the base of my dick. I watched Ronnie's toes curl every time I slammed into her body. A smile crossed my face as I thought about the effects heroin had on me when I was high. It would take me about an hour to bust a nut. And Ronnie's sneaky ass knew that, too. With one hand on her back and the thumb in her ass, I settled in for a long early morning of fucking.

***

Five hours later...
Wawas Gas Station

I needed an instant jolt of caffeine. Skipping my usual mixture of sugar and hazelnut creamer, I hit the button and let my 24 ounce cup fill up with nothing but french vanilla flavored Folgers. Walking up to the counter, I paid for the coffee and grabbed a box of glazed donuts. "That'll be 7.95, sir." The cashier said.

I tossed her a ten dollar bill, grabbed the donuts and coffee and left. Outside, I spotted the navy blue Toyota Tundra and headed towards it. I opened the passenger door and climbed into the truck. I looked at the driver of the truck and laughed. After sitting my coffee in the cup holder in the console, I opened the box of donuts and pulled one out. Greedily, I devoured it. Looking again to my left, I said, "I see you cut your beard, huh?"

"Yeah. Don't need a beard where I'm going."

"And where are you going, Sean?"

Sean Branch looked at me with a look in his eyes that I'd never seen there before.

"I'm going into the ground, but before I go, I'ma take a rack of people with me."

I reached into my pocket and pulled out a piece of paper. I passed it to Sean. "Rodney Shaw has a few different addresses in our system. They're all listed on that paper. Even the one that's on his driver's license. Was that you who killed Tony Fortune?"

Sean nodded.

"And his daughter, too?"

"It was me."

"I fuckin' knew it. Listen, I'm good at what I do. I've been the lead detective on almost every murder case that your name has been mentioned in. I do all I can to implicate you around my colleague, then I do everything I can to clean up after you when they are not around. That's the only reason you're not in jail again. And I do it because of the relationship you have with my family and the love I had for your father. The biggest threat against you was Moe Best and you took care of him. But why did you kill Trina..."

"I couldn't get Moe on my own. He knew that I wanted to bake him. So, I used Trina to get him. She was a liability at that point. So, I killed her." Sean said and shrugged. "Fuck her."

"Her son, Michael..."

"Killed him, too. Couldn't leave him around."

"Moe Best's family. Was killing them necessary?"

"It was, if one of them killed my daughter. I killed Jew Bey a couple days ago. The rest of the family is next."

"Nobody in the Best family killed Shontay. That's what I came here to tell you. But first let me fill you in on a few things. Greg Gamble is out for your blood..."

"I already know that."

"Yeah? Well, what you don't know is that Gamble has Quran Bashir's brother's cell bugged at CTF. It's completely wired for sound. And guess what? He talks too fuckin' much. On a cell phone he has, and to a friend of his named David

Battle. He's mentioned you only once that I heard, but the bug is ongoing. Who knows what he's said since I last talked to Gamble. The police in Prince George's County are building a case against your man Quran as we speak. They want to charge him with the murder of a woman named Tosheka Jennings. She was killed in the Southview Apartments on Iverson Street a month ago. They also want to charge him with the murders at the Woodmore Town Center. Why? Because his brother Jihad Bashir implicated him in those murders. Running his fuckin' mouth on the cell. You have to get word to Quran and tell him to shut up his brother's big mouth. Before he takes down the both of you. Greg Gamble thinks that we don't know where his recordings came from. But I'm smart enough to know that they came from an illegal recording device that's been planted in Jihad's cell. Do you know David Battle?"

"I know of him from Quran. But personally, naw."

"Good. Does he know anything about you?" I asked.

"Who knows, but he shouldn't. Why?

"Because his cell is probably bugged, too and ain't no telling what he's in there talking to folks about. Let's just hope that it's not you. The recording themselves can't hurt you or Quran, but like Gamble himself said, they can point all the wrong folks in the right directions. Your name has recently come up in connection to the Hayes Street murders. Six people were killed in an apartment building. You've been connected to one of the victims. Jacob Gibson. The streets call him Jakey. He was under investigation by the ATF, him and a man stationed at Bolling Air force base — correction, Andrew's man named Bernard Cullen. They knew that Cullen was selling military grade weapons to Gibson for money, drugs and young, black pussy. He had grenades, Sean. if you have those grenades and you've been using them, stop it. Some dude named Joshua Clark has also implicated you in the Byron Clark murder. Said that some fuck named Doo Doo told him that you killed Clark. And

Quran Bashir killed Artinis 'Whistle' Winston. They don't know who killed Doo Doo, real name James Yarborough, but they've connected some dots and came up with you."

"I didn't kill Doo Doo."

"Never said you did. I'm just telling you that your name came up again. It also came up in the Brion Clark murder at Stewart's. A woman was killed on the Clark family home's front porch..."

"Celine James. I thought she was Bionca Clark."

"Bionca Clark is still alive. Where she is, I don't know.if you find her and decide to kill her, be discreet. I understand that discretion is not really your forte but do it.

And I mean discreet as in whatever you did with Stephen Hartwell, Maurice Brooks and a few others. That means cool it with the hand grenades and stop cutting off people's heads. Draws too much attention. Lastly, are you familiar with a man named Von Tyler? He's dead now, but he was a notorious..."

"Killer. I'm hip to him." Sean said, his attention focused on my every word all of a sudden.

"Von Tyler has a daughter. She was the girlfriend of Brion Clark..."

"Renaissance Tyler. I'm hipped to her."

"So, you already know, then?" I asked.

Confusion etched across Sean Branch's face. "Know what?"

"That a red Infiniti SUV was parked outside the Chipotle where Shontay worked for a while. We have video footage that puts it there. The video also shows a woman exiting the Infiniti after Shontay leaves the Chipotle. The woman followed Shontay into the parking garage, then exited it minutes later. We believe that woman was Renaissance Tyler. She's the one who killed your daughter."

To be continued...

Note From the Author

Go ahead and curse me out. I know, I know. I said that part 5 would end the series, but again that was cap. You have to understand that once I get ensconced in a story, I have to tell it from every angle I see. There were too many questions left unanswered and too many plot twists to put in this one book. So, I had to extend the series one more time. The next one will be the last one, I promise. I hope that you enjoyed reading this book as much as I enjoyed writing it. I find myself in a federal penitentiary that stays on lockdown. So, that gives me too much cell time and I choose to make use of the time by writing. On another note, I want to give a soldier hug to the majority of the people I know who have navigated all the bull jive and the salt throwing in reference to me. Good men recognize a real one when they see one, so I'm proud of the men. Now with that said I gotta mention this guy named Joshua Clark. I put the guy in the book and made him a rat, but in real life he's not. Joshua Clark nicknamed Blood isn't a rat, he's a wild nigga with a rape charge. Or some type of sex charge. This coward keeps my name in his mouth repeating slander and lies. What I'm tryna understand is why good men even give the creep an audience to tear down a cold-blooded man, and he's a creep and pervert. I will never understand the NEW prison politics of today. He got checked in here where I am and he's not only allowed to walk in Beaumont USP, he's given a voice by the so-called men. All I can do is shake my head. Enough of my personal stuff. I appreciate all the support with this series and as always, all the events in this book is fiction. All of it is completely made up by the author. None of it is REAL. shout

out to all the good men in the feds, in DC jail, at Northern Neck Regional and beyond.

DC Stand up!
Buckeyfields

COMING SOON:
In The Blink of an Eye 2
If You cross Me Once 6
Ameen (The Beginning)

NOW TURN THE PAGE FOR A SNEAK PEAK AT
Angel 5: The Finale

Chapter 1
Najee

"Put the gun on the ground! Now!"
"Drop the gun, sir!"
"Put the gun down!"

I stood in the crowd and watched the scene unfold. Gunz stood not far from the Benz. the expression on his face was distant. One of his hands clutched at his side. It appeared to be covered in blood. What had happened before I walked up? Had Gunz been shot? If so, by who? I looked at Gunz as he stood there motionless. Cops were on every side of him with their guns trained on him. I wanted to call out to him. Tell him that it was over and to get down. To drop his gun and we'd find a way to get him out of this jam. But I didn't. I couldn't. I silently prayed that Gunz took one last look around and saw me standing in the crowd. But he never turned, never looked. I tried to understand what Gunz was going through as he stood there. Then his facial expression changed and it told me all that I needed to know. I watched the tears fall down Gunz's cheeks. I knew what he was going to do. A loud scream pierced the night as Gunz raised the gun and fired it at the cops. Gunshots rang out from all directions. I watched my best friend go out in a hail of bullets. Tears filled my eyes. I turned and walked away. My heart was forever broken. Gunz and Tye were gone forever. Two of the most important people in my life had died hours apart from one another. And I had no idea who was inside the Toyota. I saw the result of the crash, but it was impossible to know if the driver had been Aziz Navid or not. I walked slowly back to the Porsche. Eyes full of tears, I refused to wipe them away. I didn't care who saw my tears. My pain was on display for the whole city to see. I wanted the universe to understand that someone would die for every tear I cried. All of a sudden, a song came to mind. It played in my head with alarming clarity. As if my head was a speaker. It vibrated through my entire body...

"Day after day, seems like I push against the clouds/They just keep blocking out the sun/It seems since I was born/I wake up every blessed morning/Down on my luck and up against the wind/Don't you stop, don't you run, don't you cry/You'll do fine, you'll be good/You'll get by/Night after night, seems like I rage against the moon/But it don't never light the dark/I curse the falling rain/But it won't stop for my complaining/Down on my luck and up against the wind/Don't you run, don't you cry/

The song 'Up Against the Wind' that played out in the movie 'Set It Off' after Cleo and Frankie died was cemented inside my head and I couldn't believe the parallel circumstances that caused it to fill my head. I thought about the scene in the movie where Cleo refused to surrender and was shot down by cops. It was the exact same scene that had just played out in front of my eyes with Gunz. At the Porsche, I tried to ignore all the broken glass inside the car, the blood that stained the seat. Aminah's blood. I tried not to think about her, but I couldn't stop thinking about the fact that just like Gunz and Tye, Aminah was gone, too. I sat in the Porsche with no driver's side window to keep out the cold, I cried like a newborn baby.

Eventually, I started the car and drove through the streets of Newark. It was the city that birthed the animal in me. I realized then just how much everything had changed. Nothing was as it had been years ago. I rode past the White Castle on Elizabeth Avenue and saw it filled with dudes wearing purple bandanas. I rode past Shabazz High School and Branch Brook Park skating rink. The past could never return to confront the present. And the future was a naked bitch walking to and fro, uncertain of where she was headed. The cold wind that smacked me in the face as I drove couldn't keep my tears from staining my cheeks. The end of my journey found me right back where it started. Brick Towers. Yellow crime scene tape cordoned off the area where Aminah's body had been. Where I had left it. Plain clothed and uniformed officers were still at the scene. I parked the Porsche and then proceeded to the projects on foot. Minutes later, police cars swarmed the area out of nowhere. Marked and unmarked. The cops leapt out of the cars and surrounded me. A black detective that I knew personally emerged from the crowd.

"Take your hands out your pockets, Najee." Detective Curtis Dobbs said. "And get down on your knees and put your hands on your head. If you do anything other than what I just said, we'll shoot you."

I did as instructed and complied completely with every command. I was frisked and the gun I carried was taken off my waist. As I was being handcuffed, I tried to remember all that I had done with the gun. It was clean as far as I could remember. Lifted from the ground, I was led to a nearby squad car. The detective I knew walked up and said, "Najee Bashir, you're under arrest for the murder of Richard Giles. You have the right to remain silent. Anything you say can and will be used against you in a court of law..."

***

Later that day...
After the processing, I was placed in a large holding cell. One that I hadn't been in since being arrested for shoplifting as a teenager. I pulled off my coat, balled it up and used it as a pillow on the metal bench. Laying there, I thought about what the cop had said. I was charged with killing Richard Giles. Without having to be told, I knew that Richard Giles was 'Rich', the dude me and Gunz bodied at the gas station. The murder must've been caught on video.

"Najee Bashir?" A voice called out.

I opened my eyes and looked up to see an Asian detective at the bars. "Yeah, what's good, yo?"

"Wanna step up here for a moment?"

"Naw. Talk."

"Do you wanna talk about what you're charged with?"

"Naw. I'm good."

The detective left quickly and minutes later, a uniformed lady cop appeared. "Bashir, come on, you get a phone call."

I was released from the holding cage and let to a phone. I dialed a number I had remembered by heart. It was answered on the second ring. "Carlos?"

"Najee?"

"Yeah, it's me. What's good, pops? I'm in a jam. I'm in jail for murder."

"When did you get arrested?"

"This morning."

"So, you're still at the police station?"

"Yeah, I'm about to be transported to the Essex County Correctional facility. Then tomorrow, I got to court."

"Okay, just sit tight and be cool. I'm sending someone up there today. They'll be at your court hearing. I'ma get you out of there, so don't sweat anything. No worries. Do you need anything else besides freedom?

"Naw, I'm good, but Gunz and Tye ain't."

"Are they in jail, too?"

"Naw, they're dead. And Aziz ain't."

"Say no more. Call when you get to Essex County."

"I will. Let Angel know where I am."

"I will. Talk to you later, son. Let me get the ball rolling."

"Aight, pops. One."

***

Essex County jail
354 Doremus Avenue
Newark, NJ

"Gentleman, welcome to the Green Monster. Take off all of your clothes and form a single file line. As you pass through this door here, stop and stand in front of an officer. That officer will search you. If you have any contraband on you, please leave it in this room somewhere. Because if we find it once you go through this door, we are going to beat your fuckin' ass. Understood, gentlemen?"

No one in the room spoke up and said a word.

"Okay, good." The correctional officer said. "Now, strip!"

***

"Najee Bashir?" A man called out.

"Right here." I replied.

"Step in that room over there and see the lieutenant."

I stepped into a small room and saw an officer seated at a table.

"Sit down, Bashir. I'm Lieutenant Tafuri."

"I sat in the seat across from the lieutenant.

"Where are you from in Newark, Bashir?" Lt. Tafuri asked.

"Brick Towers."

"Brick Towers?" The lieutenant repeated and wrote down what I said. "And what gang are you affiliated with?"

"None."

"No gang?"

I shook my head. "No gang."

"Religion?"

"Muslim."

"Figures. Well, Mr. Najee, I've read your arrest report and you have the unfortunate luck of being charged with the murder of Richard Giles. Everybody here was familiar with Rich. But we are even more familiar with Richar Giles' brother. Mosekilah Stafford also known as Homicide. Homicide is the leader of the largest gang housed in this facility. The Grape Street Crips. Richard Giles and Masekilah Stafford are both from the Baxter Terrace projects. Which also boast another 100 or so inmates who are not Crips, but love to put on for the hood. These inmates are housed all over the facility and I can't let them kill you here. So, unfortunately, you'll be going to 2C1, the Protective Custody Unit..."

"I'd rather die."

"Is that right, Bashir?"

"It's death before dishonor. Always."

"If you're refusing protective custody, you gotta sign off on it."

"Where's the paperwork I gotta sign?"

"I'm gonna get it for you, Najee. And for what it's worth, I respect your decision. But it's your funeral. Wait here..."

Stay tuned for Angel 5: The Finale Coming Soon

Lock Down Publications and Ca$h Presents
Assisted Publishing Packages

BASIC PACKAGE $499 Editing Cover Design Formatting	UPGRADED PACKAGE $800 Typing Editing Cover Design Formatting
ADVANCE PACKAGE $1,200 Typing Editing Cover Design Formatting Copyright registration Proofreading Upload book to Amazon	LDP SUPREME PACKAGE $1,500 Typing Editing Cover Design Formatting Copyright registration Proofreading Set up Amazon account Upload book to Amazon Advertise on LDP, Amazon and Facebook Page

***Other services available upon request.
Additional charges may apply

Lock Down Publications
P.O. Box 944
Stockbridge, GA 30281-9998
Phone: 470 303-9761

Submission Guideline

Submit the first three chapters of your completed manuscript to ldpsubmissions@gmail.com. In the subject line add **Your Book's Title**. The manuscript must be in a Word Doc file and sent as an attachment. Document should be in Times New Roman, double spaced, and in size 12 font. Also, provide your synopsis and full contact information. If sending multiple submissions, they must each be in a separate email.

Have a story but no way to send it electronically? You can still submit to LDP/Ca$h Presents. Send in the first three chapters, written or typed, of your completed manuscript to:

LDP: Submissions Dept
P.O. Box 944
Stockbridge, GA 30281-9998

DO NOT send original manuscript. Must be a duplicate.
Provide your synopsis and a cover letter containing your full contact information.

Thanks for considering LDP and Ca$h Presents.

NEW RELEASES

BLOODLINE OF A SAVAGE 1&2
THESE VICIOUS STREETS 1&2
RELENTLESS GOON
RELENTLESS GOON 2
BY PRINCE A. TAUHID

THE BUTTERFLY MAFIA 1-3
BY FUMIYA PAYNE

A THUG'S STREET PRINCESS 1&2
BY MEESHA

CITY OF SMOKE 2
BY MOLOTTI

STEPPERS 1,2&3
THE REAL BADDIES OF CHI-RAQ
BY KING RIO

THE LANE 1&2
BY KEN-KEN SPENCE

THUG OF SPADES 1&2
LOVE IN THE TRENCHES 2
CORNER BOYS
BY COREY ROBINSON

TIL DEATH 3
BY ARYANNA

THE BIRTH OF A GANGSTER 4
BY DELMONT PLAYER

PRODUCT OF THE STREETS 1&2
BY DEMOND "MONEY" ANDERSON

NO TIME FOR ERROR
BY KEESE

MONEY HUNGRY DEMONS
BY TRANAY ADAMS

Coming Soon from Lock Down Publications/Ca$h Presents

IF YOU CROSS ME ONCE 6
ANGEL V
By Anthony Fields

IMMA DIE BOUT MINE 5
By Aryanna

A THUGS STREET PRINCESS 3
By Meesha

PRODUCT OF THE STREETS 3
By Demond Money Anderson

CORNER BOYS 2
By Corey Robinson

THE MURDER QUEENS 6&7
By Michael Gallon

CITY OF SMOKE 3
By Molotti

CONFESSIONS OF A DOPE BOY
By Nicholas Lock

THA TAKEOVER
By Keith Chandler

BETRAYAL OF A G 2
By Ray Vinci

CRIME BOSS
By Playa Ray

Available Now

RESTRAINING ORDER 1 & 2
By **CA$H & Coffee**

LOVE KNOWS NO BOUNDARIES 1-3
By **Coffee**

RAISED AS A GOON I, II, III & IV
BRED BY THE SLUMS I, II, III
BLAST FOR ME I & II
ROTTEN TO THE CORE I II III
A BRONX TALE I, II, III
DUFFLE BAG CARTEL I II III IV V VI
HEARTLESS GOON I II III IV V
A SAVAGE DOPEBOY I II
DRUG LORDS I II III
CUTTHROAT MAFIA I II
KING OF THE TRENCHES
By **Ghost**

LAY IT DOWN I & II
LAST OF A DYING BREED I II
BLOOD STAINS OF A SHOTTA I & II III
By **Jamaica**

LOYAL TO THE GAME I II III
LIFE OF SIN I, II III
By **TJ & Jelissa**

IF LOVING HIM IS WRONG…I & II
LOVE ME EVEN WHEN IT HURTS I II III
By **Jelissa**

PUSH IT TO THE LIMIT
By **Bre' Hayes**

BLOODY COMMAS I & II
SKI MASK CARTEL I, II & III
KING OF NEW YORK I II, III IV V
RISE TO POWER I II III
COKE KINGS I II III IV V
BORN HEARTLESS I II III IV
KING OF THE TRAP I II
By **T.J. Edwards**

WHEN THE STREETS CLAP BACK I & II III
THE HEART OF A SAVAGE I II III IV
MONEY MAFIA I II
LOYAL TO THE SOIL I II III
By **Jibril Williams**

A DISTINGUISHED THUG STOLE MY HEART I II & III
LOVE SHOULDN'T HURT I II III IV
RENEGADE BOYS 1-4
PAID IN KARMA 1-3
SAVAGE STORMS 1-3
AN UNFORESEEN LOVE 1-3
BABY, I'M WINTERTIME COLD 1-3
A THUG'S STREET PRINCESS 1&2
By **Meesha**

A GANGSTER'S CODE 1-3
A GANGSTER'S SYN 1-3
THE SAVAGE LIFE 1-3
CHAINED TO THE STREETS 1-3
BLOOD ON THE MONEY 1-3
A GANGSTA'S PAIN 1-3
BEAUTIFUL LIES AND UGLY TRUTHS
CHURCH IN THESE STREETS
By **J-Blunt**

CUM FOR ME 1-8
An LDP Erotica Collaboration

BLOOD OF A BOSS 1-5
SHADOWS OF THE GAME
TRAP BASTARD
By **Askari**

THE STREETS BLEED MURDER 1-3
THE HEART OF A GANGSTA 1-3
By **Jerry Jackson**

WHEN A GOOD GIRL GOES BAD
By **Adrienne**

THE COST OF LOYALTY 1-3
By **Kweli**

BRIDE OF A HUSTLA 1-3
THE FETTI GIRLS 1-3
CORRUPTED BY A GANGSTA 1-4
BLINDED BY HIS LOVE
THE PRICE YOU PAY FOR LOVE 1-3
DOPE GIRL MAGIC 1-3
By **Destiny Skai**

A KINGPIN'S AMBITION
A KINGPIN'S AMBITION II
I MURDER FOR THE DOUGH
By **Ambitious**

TRUE SAVAGE 1-7
DOPE BOY MAGIC 1-3
MIDNIGHT CARTEL 1-3
CITY OF KINGZ 1&2
NIGHTMARE ON SILENT AVE
THE PLUG OF LIL MEXICO 1&2
CLASSIC CITY
By **Chris Green**

A GANGSTER'S REVENGE 1-4
THE BOSS MAN'S DAUGHTERS 1-5
A SAVAGE LOVE 1&2
BAE BELONGS TO ME 1&2
A HUSTLER'S DECEIT 1-3
WHAT BAD BITCHES DO 1-3
SOUL OF A MONSTER 1-3
KILL ZONE
A DOPE BOY'S QUEEN 1-3
TIL DEATH 1-3
IMMA DIE BOUT MINE 1-4
By **Aryanna**

A DOPEBOY'S PRAYER
By **Eddie "Wolf" Lee**

THE KING CARTEL 1-3
By **Frank Gresham**

THESE NIGGAS AIN'T LOYAL 1-3
By **Nikki Tee**

GANGSTA SHYT 1-3
By **CATO**

THE ULTIMATE BETRAYAL
By **Phoenix**

BOSS'N UP 1-3
By **Royal Nicole**

I LOVE YOU TO DEATH
By **Destiny J**

I RIDE FOR MY HITTA
I STILL RIDE FOR MY HITTA
By **Misty Holt**

LOVE & CHASIN' PAPER
By **Qay Crockett**

TO DIE IN VAIN
SINS OF A HUSTLA
By **ASAD**

BROOKLYN HUSTLAZ
By **Boogsy Morina**

BROOKLYN ON LOCK 1 & 2
By **Sonovia**

GANGSTA CITY
By **Teddy Duke**

A DRUG KING AND HIS DIAMOND 1-3
A DOPEMAN'S RICHES
HER MAN, MINE'S TOO 1&2
CASH MONEY HO'S
THE WIFEY I USED TO BE 1&2
PRETTY GIRLS DO NASTY THINGS
By **Nicole Goosby**

LIPSTICK KILLAH 1-3
CRIME OF PASSION 1-3
FRIEND OR FOE 1-3
By **Mimi**

TRAPHOUSE KING 1-3
KINGPIN KILLAZ 1-3
STREET KINGS 1&2
PAID IN BLOOD 1&2
CARTEL KILLAZ 1-3
DOPE GODS 1&2
By **Hood Rich**

THE STREETS ARE CALLING
By **Duquie Wilson**

STEADY MOBBN' 1-3
THE STREETS STAINED MY SOUL 1-3
By **Marcellus Allen**

WHO SHOT YA 1-3
SON OF A DOPE FIEND 1-4
HEAVEN GOT A GHETTO 1&2
SKI MASK MONEY 1&2
By **Renta**

GORILLAZ IN THE BAY 1-4
TEARS OF A GANGSTA 1/&2
3X KRAZY 1&2
STRAIGHT BEAST MODE 1&2
By **DE'KARI**

TRIGGADALE 1-3
MURDA WAS THE CASE 1-3
By **Elijah R. Freeman**

SLAUGHTER GANG 1-3
RUTHLESS HEART 1-3
By **Willie Slaughter**

GOD BLESS THE TRAPPERS 1-3
THESE SCANDALOUS STREETS 1-3
FEAR MY GANGSTA 1-5
THESE STREETS DON'T LOVE NOBODY 1-2
BURY ME A G 1-5
A GANGSTA'S EMPIRE 1-4
THE DOPEMAN'S BODYGAURD 1&2
THE REALEST KILLAZ 1-3
THE LAST OF THE OGS 1-3
By **Tranay Adams**

MARRIED TO A BOSS 1-3
By **Destiny Skai & Chris Green**

KINGZ OF THE GAME 1-7
CRIME BOSS 1-3
By **Playa Ray**

FUK SHYT
By **Blakk Diamond**

DON'T F#CK WITH MY HEART 1&2
By **Linnea**

ADDICTED TO THE DRAMA 1-3
IN THE ARM OF HIS BOSS
By **Jamila**

LOYALTY AIN'T PROMISED 1&2
By **Keith Williams**

YAYO 1-4
A SHOOTER'S AMBITION 1&2
BRED IN THE GAME
By **S. Allen**

TRAP GOD 1-3
RICH $AVAGE 1-3
MONEY IN THE GRAVE 1-3
CARTEL MONEY
By **Martell Troublesome Bolden**

FOREVER GANGSTA 1&2
GLOCKS ON SATIN SHEETS 1&2
By **Adrian Dulan**

TOE TAGZ 1-4
LEVELS TO THIS SHYT 1&2
IT'S JUST ME AND YOU
By **Ah'Million**

IF YOU CROSS ME ONCE 5 | ANTHONY FIELDS

KINGPIN DREAMS 1-3
RAN OFF ON DA PLUG
By **Paper Boi Rari**

THE STREETS MADE ME 1-3
By **Larry D. Wright**

CONFESSIONS OF A GANGSTA 1-4
CONFESSIONS OF A JACKBOY 1-3
CONFESSIONS OF A HITMAN
By **Nicholas Lock**

I'M NOTHING WITHOUT HIS LOVE
SINS OF A THUG
TO THE THUG I LOVED BEFORE
A GANGSTA SAVED XMAS
IN A HUSTLER I TRUST
By **Monet Dragun**

QUIET MONEY 1-3
THUG LIFE 1-3
EXTENDED CLIP 1&2
A GANGSTA'S PARADISE
By **Trai'Quan**

CAUGHT UP IN THE LIFE 1-3
THE STREETS NEVER LET GO 1-3
By **Robert Baptiste**

NEW TO THE GAME 1-3
MONEY, MURDER & MEMORIES 1-3
By **Malik D. Rice**

CREAM 2-3
THE STREETS WILL TALK
By **Yolanda Moore**

THE STREETS WILL NEVER CLOSE 1-3
By **K'ajji**

210

LIFE OF A SAVAGE 1-4
A GANGSTA'S QUR'AN 1-4
MURDA SEASON 1-3
GANGLAND CARTEL 1-3
CHI'RAQ GANGSTAS 1-4
KILLERS ON ELM STREET 1-3
JACK BOYZ N DA BRONX 1-3
A DOPEBOY'S DREAM 1-3
JACK BOYS VS DOPE BOYS 1-3
COKE GIRLZ
COKE BOYS
SOSA GANG 1&2
BRONX SAVAGES
BODYMORE KINGPINS
BLOOD OF A GOON
By **Romell Tukes**

CONCRETE KILLA 1-3
VICIOUS LOYALTY 1-3
By **Kingpen**

THE ULTIMATE SACRIFICE 1-6
KHADIFI
IF YOU CROSS ME ONCE 1-3
ANGEL 1-4
IN THE BLINK OF AN EYE
By **Anthony Fields**

THE LIFE OF A HOOD STAR
By **Ca$h & Rashia Wilson**

NIGHTMARES OF A HUSTLA 1-3
BLOOD AND GAMES 1&2
By **King Dream**

GHOST MOB
By **Stilloan Robinson**

HARD AND RUTHLESS 1&2
MOB TOWN 251
THE BILLIONAIRE BENTLEYS 1-3
REAL G'S MOVE IN SILENCE
By **Von Diesel**

MOB TIES 1-7
SOUL OF A HUSTLER, HEART OF A KILLER 1-3
GORILLAZ IN THE TRENCHES
By **SayNoMore**

BODYMORE MURDERLAND 1-3
THE BIRTH OF A GANGSTER 1-4
By **Delmont Player**

FOR THE LOVE OF A BOSS 1&2
By **C. D. Blue**

KILLA KOUNTY 1-5
By **Khufu**

MOBBED UP 1-4
THE BRICK MAN 1-5
THE COCAINE PRINCESS 1-10
STEPPERS 1-3
SUPER GREMLIN 1-4
By **King Rio**

MONEY GAME 1&2
By **Smoove Dolla**

A GANGSTA'S KARMA 1-4
By **FLAME**

KING OF THE TRENCHES 1-3
By **GHOST & TRANAY ADAMS**

IF YOU CROSS ME ONCE 5 | ANTHONY FIELDS

QUEEN OF THE ZOO 1&2
By **Black Migo**

GRIMEY WAYS 1-3
BETRAYAL OF A G
By **Ray Vinci**

XMAS WITH AN ATL SHOOTER
By **Ca$h & Destiny Skai**

KING KILLA 1&2
By **Vincent "Vitto" Holloway**

BETRAYAL OF A THUG 1&2
By **Fre$h**

THE MURDER QUEENS 1-5
By **Michael Gallon**

FOR THE LOVE OF BLOOD 1-4
By **Jamel Mitchell**

HOOD CONSIGLIERE 1&2
NO TIME FOR ERROR
By **Keese**

PROTÉGÉ OF A LEGEND 1&2
LOVE IN THE TRENCHES 1&2
By **Corey Robinson**

THE PLUG'S RUTHLESS DAUGHTER
By **Tony Daniels**

BORN IN THE GRAVE 1-3
CRIME PAYS
By **Self Made Tay**

MOAN IN MY MOUTH
By **XTASY**

TORN BETWEEN A GANGSTER AND A GENTLEMAN
By **J-BLUNT & Miss Kim**

LOYALTY IS EVERYTHING 1-3
CITY OF SMOKE 1&2
By **Molotti**

HERE TODAY GONE TOMORROW 1&2
By **Fly Rock**

WOMEN LIE MEN LIE 1-4
FIFTY SHADES OF SNOW 1-3
STACK BEFORE YOU SPLURGE
GIRLS FALL LIKE DOMINOES
NAÏVE TO THE STREETS
By **ROY MILLIGAN**

PILLOW PRINCESS
By **S. Hawkins**

THE BUTTERFLY MAFIA 1-3
SALUTE MY SAVAGERY 1&2
By **Fumiya Payne**

THE LANE 1&2
By Ken-Ken Spence

THE PUSSY TRAP 1-5
By **Nene Capri**

DIRTY DNA
By **Blaque**

SANCTIFIED AND HORNY
by **XTASY**

BOOKS BY LDP'S CEO, CA$H

TRUST IN NO MAN
TRUST IN NO MAN 2
TRUST IN NO MAN 3
BONDED BY BLOOD
SHORTY GOT A THUG
THUGS CRY
THUGS CRY 2
THUGS CRY 3
TRUST NO BITCH
TRUST NO BITCH 2
TRUST NO BITCH 3
TIL MY CASKET DROPS
RESTRAINING ORDER
RESTRAINING ORDER 2
IN LOVE WITH A CONVICT
LIFE OF A HOOD STAR
XMAS WITH AN ATL SHOOTER

Printed in the USA
CPSIA information can be obtained
at www.ICGtesting.com
LVHW021717031024
792833LV00002B/202

9 781965 448007